I've Got Tickets
to Heaven

Just need to call for a limousine

JC de Melo

Published by BookLocker.com, Inc., St. Petersburg, Florida.

The characters and events in this book are fictitious. Any similarity to real persons, living or dead, is coincidental and not intended by the author.

Printed on acid-free paper.

Library of Congress Cataloging in Publication Data
De Melo, JC
I'VE GOT TICKETS TO HEAVEN: Just Need to
Call for a Limousine by JC de Melo
Library of Congress Control Number: 2020908007

BookLocker.com, Inc.
2020

Cover designed by DP Designs.

To no one in particular.

Or all humans who existed in the past,

exist now and will come to exist in the future

Disclaimer

This novel, like any other story, is a product of pure fiction. It has come to exist only to satisfy my desire to add value to the conversation of religion or non-religion, of heaven or of no existence of such place; and above all, of God's presence in our lives. Or any other type of divine creation that has been debated for centuries by all theological and philosophical minds. Well, ask Einstein.

Possessing no degrees or background in any of the essential credentials, my coming to the conversation is then for pure pedestrian or street conversation. Yes, we all talk about issues that, in spite of being under the domain of doctors of some kind, are fundamental to our existence and the right to believe. We are, after all, some sort of experts in one matter or another. Just being alive, observing well, does grant us the right to add to the argument.

There are many aspects, details of the stories and dialogues that may give the appearance of veracity or real-live experiences. They are not. With rare exceptions and in part with the exception of the Author's notes, they do not reflect real experiences of any kind. My imagination then was and is now at work.

Enjoy the ride!

JC de Melo

Table of Contents

Author's

Initial Notes
&
Message

*Jesus addressed this parable to those that were
convinced of their own righteousness and despised
everyone else: "Two people went up to the temple area
to pray; one was a Pharisee and the other a Tax
Collector. The Pharisee took up his position and spoke
this prayer to himself,
'O God, I thank you that I am not like the rest of
humanity - greedy, dishonest, adulterous - or even like
this tax collector. I fast twice a week, and I pay tithes
on my whole income.'
But the tax collector stood off at a distance and would
not even raise his eyes to heaven but beat his breast
and prayed, 'O God, be merciful to me, a sinner.'
I tell you, the latter went home justified, not the
former; for whoever exalts himself will be humbled,
and the one who humbles himself will be exalted."
(Bible - Luke 18:9-14)*

Sometimes it is complicated living in our own planet. A "Catch twenty-two" is also many times what we get for doing one thing or not the other. We cannot get a break. Add the condition of being a Christian believer and the odds against you move up a few notches. Add another notch if you are Catholic. That notch comes in the form of guilt --- and nobody that I know does the guilt dance as Catholics do. Perhaps confession still prevails in Catholic doctrine for those where the guilt requires some soothing, a washing away of the guilt for at least a few hours. Certainly, it is a humbling and necessary undertaking.

What unfolds next is just a few *fictional* experiences that can encapsulate what we do not fully know about our destiny after our own and unique mission in our planet is over, is done. Unless we have the power to come back again disguised or under some other form. How did we do? Who were we? The Pharisee or the tax collector --- the despised traitor of his own clan? Were we (most likely) **both** at the same time or at one time or another? Or what role did we play in the movie "Trading Places:" the homeless and beggar or the arrogant and selfish businessmen?

Fast forward ….

…. C'mon God, I've lived a righteous life, gave money to the church and charity, paid the minimum wage stipulated by government, said nice things at least to some of my neighbors, I smiled at those that smiled at me and... I am not justified? Really?

God, you know me better than I know myself. But what I know is that I have not lived a good life: I have cheated on some of my friends, or even on my customers, could have avoided compromising situations; in a small sentence, I have lived the life of a "scum-bag." In my mind I deserve no forgiveness. Yet, You have the last word….

∞∞∞∞∞

With the thousands or millions of books and research done by people considered competent or credentialed on the matter, I still do not know or no one for that matter does know the final outcome of any particular human life or the life after we say goodbye to our planet. We just don't. Granted, lots of arguments and dissertations come from both sides --- the believers and non-believers. It is what it is.

With way over seven billion humans in our planet today, and still growing exponentially every day, one can refer to any source of information found in encyclopedias, Google, Wikipedia, Encyclopedia Britannica, etc. and learn that not every one of the seven plus billion is religious or has a defined conviction on the true existence of God or any other Divine being. Depending on who is doing the counting, close to two and one half billion are considered Christians, another number close to two billion is said to be Muslims and another two billion belonging to Eastern deities. The rest, let's do the counting one more time --- one and one half billion do not profess any religion and thus do not believe that God exists or has any meaning in our daily lives. And taking into account that many listed in any religious group do not practice their religion as one should endeavor to, the numbers tend to favor those who have no need to talk about or engage in religious conversations. At least these are all even --- living their lives with no discerning obligation to adhere to this or that church, church leader or doctrine. Nevertheless, they are as engaged in acts of charity, kindness, solidarity with the world or, above all, living upstanding lives. And narrowing their numbers to my own life some of them are my friends and people whom I trust with absolute plenitude. They are my friends, perhaps were my bosses or my subordinates, school mates and community engaged neighbors.

Born and raised Catholic was for me a gift that is shared by millions. Still Catholic, more mature from living over seven decades, dedicating more time to endeavors close to the heart and soul, and having more time to contemplate the whole meaning of living, the presence of God in my life and those around me is firmer now than at any time before. Thus, I am lucky for all kinds of reasons. Others who have died much younger missed the opportunities that I have had to read more, to learn more, to investigate more, to reflect on the meaning of God and perhaps heaven and hell. Because I was allowed to live long, I guess to know more, question more, dialogue more, may not automatically grant me preferred treatment or the best seat in the house -- supposedly in heaven. Whatever vision of heaven anyone has. The fact that a niece died at age forty-four, a brother-in-law died at age sixty-two may not be indicative that they missed the boat or the train to heaven. Another fact that astonished me the other day was recollecting that my mother passed away at the age of twenty-one. How much did she know about God or his designed outcomes on any human being? Why twenty-one? I was told she was a very nice lady, talented within the world of little then, good looking (I have pictures of her) and vivacious. Great basic traits to influence me in some manner; yet, it did not happen. Was heaven offered to her? I hope it was and that she was excited with that possibility. In contrast, my father died at age eighty-eight and lived a decent life. He was also borderline religious to the point that he traded, on his last twenty years, give or take a year, Catholicism for Witnesses of Jehovah. He was an Elder at the time of his passing away. I presume it was a good position. As opposed to my mother, did he have a privilege that she did not have? Did he buy tickets to heaven? For, as a Witness of Jehovah, he had, together with over two hundred thousand witnesses, exclusive rights to heaven. Or so we are told. The others, perhaps like me, may have to find a way by foot. Mind you, he was a good man, took care of his family and treated people well. Nevertheless, this last observation is my thesis for second guessing his late-in-life beliefs and ultimate decision. Not one, even the known saints of the Church, knew for sure how it all works. One thing I believe unequivocally, is that God, the maker of heaven and earth (for those who believe) would not waste his time and talent to create us in His image to later on send us to waste in no man's land. It does not make sense. Well, there are some others, who by choice, elect not to do good. Hence, they refuse God's many gifts or offers of grace.

Certainly, the privilege to see God's face is not for us to know. We just do not know. Instead practice good deeds; beyond those that are convenient! Then let Him decide. Amen!

JC de Melo

1

Max

I could almost read my future

It is more valuable to God to have a caring,
loveable and engaged Atheist,
than a hypocrite Christian
-----Pope Francis

I knew there was something special about me. I just knew it. That thought, on the borderline of full conviction, was (crystal) clear, at least during those last months in the warm and bouncing world of Mom's womb. I was not scared; as I became aware that all stages of my life would be challenging, perhaps complex. But, in the end, they would be relevant and destiny driven. Even in my last days of residence inside my mother's womb, I could feel some trouble coming right after my birth and envisioned a future that would entail some controversy between my father and my grandfather. Although both nearly espoused the same beliefs, each one would address the controversy somewhat differently. Same DNAs but different eras and environments, not to mention different generations -- would dictate inherent or modified behaviors. One would live with his beliefs intact, unaltered, and the other would not. Actually, my father would second-guess himself on these beliefs at the very end of his breathing on earth. Those outcomes would become troublesome for me at times or energize me towards chasing more answers. Uneasy feelings with shades of affliction would follow me, would disturb my inner and outward peace. Thus, because I loved both dearly, I became determined to commence my own mission towards explaining to myself first, and then to those I would mingle with later, why we did what we did in life.

Whether an agreement had been drafted or not, residence in my mom's womb was for the full term -- nine months and one day. There was no charge for that extra day! At that price, I would stay as long as I wished or as long as my mom's residence would tolerate her discomfort. As I grew in my mom's tummy, the waters in the amniotic bag would slowly trickle to an end; and thus, the comfort in mom and me would also vanish. Friction would make our lives somewhat miserable. Of course, I never inquired how long one could live in a mom's womb. I wish I had stayed longer in my mom's tummy and, for certain, to finally win the battle with the umbilical cord. The cord, that precious vehicle for my nourishment, was about to win, perhaps a second or two after I was kicked out of my living arrangement through the tunnel and directed to the world of the earthlings. Unbeknownst to or unfelt by the obstetrician (the interested party) and his assistants, the cord stayed tightly wrapped around my neck more than one time. Mostly, because I had played with it -- like rock climbing -- a little too much in the last moments or until I was ready to come out. Certainly, my actions fooled the practitioner, causing an erroneous reading that I was fine. It was too late for me to regret I had gone too far with my play. The result was that, despite the doctor's Herculean effort to free the knot from my neck, much oxygen had been lost. I was not still-borne. I was brain unconscious or brain damaged. Hence, change from the bouncing and comfortable mom's tummy to some other residence -- foreign to me -- was not auspicious. Going from a controlled floating to a padded, but static environment did not help at all. I was officially out, but equally officially almost unimportant, inconsequential or ultimately irrelevant. Subsequently, I could not advance my life on earth as other babies did; because while the others had a brain in normal motion, mine was mostly shut off. Until the eleventh day, when the doctors were about to pronounce that my short stay was over -- it was inconsequential.

Just then, mysteriously (perhaps miraculously), I was given a second chance. For clarification, the word miracle had never fared well in our small family of father, mother, sister and grandparents. My grandfather, alone, would almost go ballistic if the word was uttered by any one of us by mistake or just in casual talking. Indeed, that was just one of a few other nouns and adjectives he unceremoniously detested. If in my growing years I was conscious about their meaning and their place in life, later on, I became totally immunized to any effects of words or meanings of supernatural, spiritual tones and their consequences. In good faith, in my grandfather's household, even when the bets were off and there was a winner, it was not viewed as a simple and innocent miracle. It was a product of science still unknown to humans. After all, the word was not important, for my circle of friends was no more than two. Certainly, I do not recall conversations on miracles or related matters. Our family life style was normally private and friendly but with invisible frontiers. My grandfather was a part-time professor (more a lecturer than teacher), a journalist and an active-behind-the-scenes political agitator. I did not coin the phrase. My grandfather did the honors when answering a particular question from my mother. "How can you be a behind-the-lines political agitator? By the very essence of politics, one cannot be an invisible agitator. In politics?" Then he answered with the same authority and determination: "Yes I can say I am an agitator behind the lines. Rarely putting my signature on ideas or making perilous comments on any absurd state of the nation." My grandfather was no coward or hypocrite. Yet, knowing that the political waters of his era were at times agitated and that misinterpreting different points of view would land his well-weaved reputation into chaos -- like being seen and thus labeled a communist. McCarthyism was not pleasant for some professions or professors.

So, I survived, barely, on the twelfth day after my very brief contact with other living creatures in the world. On those days, there were no special tools to evaluate the conditions or the environment inside my mom's lodge. Some ultrasound exams or internal pictures were not available; only my own breathing and my mom's nonchalant chats with the doctor revealed that there were no breaches in my marathon of doing nothing -- eat, drink and sleep. On that twelfth day, I was too weak to move to my parents. It was on that célèbre transition from the eleventh to the twelfth day that the first sign that I would be different came to my own door. While all hopes that I would survive were about to go away, a nurse on her routine duties, casually reminded my parents that a religious minister was in the vicinity of our ward and invited them to avail of his spiritual and healing credentials. My father was a polite human being. Actually, I never observed him in the years ahead to be less than civilized and with a balanced temper. Rather than telling the nurse to mind her own business and shove her advice into an appropriate anatomic place, he smiled and just uttered his familiar *"thank you."* His eyes never met the nurse's eyes and his voice was meek; but his message of gratitude was unequivocal. Years later, in my early teens, that episode came to surface in a flash back conversation with my grandfather. I remember what he said: "Reginald, too bad I was not around then. I would strangle that nurse's neck for pitching such voodoo medicine -- a spiritual prayer, a moment of recognition of God's existence. And what did you tell the nurse?" continued my grandfather. My father just told him the truth: "Thanks. We have our own way of consoling ourselves." My father then added that, in the few days that followed the episode, he politely avoided the nurse as much as possible. He preferred silence to any potential confrontation with my grandfather. By then, I had been transferred to another ward. My destiny would take its own predictable turn.

∞∞∞∞∞

Now I am definitely at a very serious crossroads in my life. I cannot deny it. Much less can I continue to inflict some pain on me and on those that love me so much. Never mind I anticipated that eventually I would bang my head onto a reality that was inevitable. Never mind that my own traits and qualities would sell me away as one that owned beliefs behind a façade that had been perpetuated too long or were not my own. Never mind that my promise to my dad could have produced the same second guess as his own, or eventually discover that my grandfather was wrong about his own views and beliefs. Never mind that he never gave himself a chance to allow the truth to find peace with his own character. Never mind that there are still many questions difficult to answer. Never mind that millions of minds continue to play with fire -- free thinking, continuous denials and cover-ups. Never mind that all would be perhaps so simple if only one would allow innocence to flourish and gain hold. Well, ask my uncle Frederick, or maybe Vera, or Walt, or Fausto or Herbert or, above all, Sam. Sam for sure! He was so different than all of us and yet, so close -- we were all human beings with identical (but inside) personal missions. This "crossroads" does not intimidate me now nor propels me to dig even more on the unknown, or on what is disputed by all sides of the existence or non-existence of God. I am comfortable being a more enlightened on-the-fence believer of all or nothing. I love my uncle Frederick. I still feel his distant influence, his neutrality to philosophic arguments, his acceptance that what he knew was warm and what he did not know was good enough to attain his peace of mind. His life was so relevant as my father's was. It is just that my father was peaceful but also colorless. My uncle Frederick, my father's brother, was very colorful, influential and invisibly serene. His children, and my cousins said so at their farewell message during his funeral services. I remember it well. I will revisit those moments, I will. Yet, I am thinking of Vera now. She has made some good points that have grown on me.

∞∞∞∞∞

In spite of the fervor from the Christian right towards political arenas, the atheist community is actually growing. They are staunch followers of their own doctrine that does not impose any moral sanctions or invoke old covenants. They claim that delving into spiritual forests causes much stress, or trying to figure out the meaning of God, causes more agony than just leaving it alone, untouched, unexplored, unexperienced. That in itself sets the tone for their claim of being relevant as to being also guardians of human rights and siding with efforts towards equalization of opportunities; leveling the playing field. Contrary to what these Christians think, most atheists do not espouse nihilistic views, or live very sad lives. Hence, they do not channel their energies in proving what they think no one has yet proved, or beyond any doubts.

"Okay, Max, I get the point and find myself, in part, agreeing with that doctrine," replied Elvera. That initial statement by the speaker, together with the other insights, makes a point in justifying the moderate but provable growth of atheism."

Max found himself drawn to the conversation in spite of his reluctance to address matters that would elevate the discussion towards hot arguments or in the end to the resignation that no one won any unfriendly contest. Thus, causing each one to retire to their comfort zones certain that there was more futility than enlightenment. He was not a bit surprised that Elvera started the conversation with the basic bullet statement with which the speaker, an apparent atheist, initiated his brief but almost eloquent presentation.

"Vera, yours is a good invitation for dialogue. However, you know where I stand on the issue. Since we have been together in our organization, we spoke on what we believe, what we care, where we had come from and how we conduct our lives. We never let our (inner and stronger) beliefs be in the way of doing what we agreed to do. Once we learned the rules of the game, we just concentrated on deeds and actions and not dogmas. I respect you dearly but that is the way I think. Although Atheism is not a religion, in the context of his presentation, the speaker did highlight it as being such. He presented his views with coherence, showed some statistics, elevated the deeds of many folks in our society who are staunch atheists and underlined the rationale for following their cause. They are smacked in the middle of our society's needs and urges, and interests. Yet, I prefer not to go there."

Max noted that Walter, right across from him, by his body language, was becoming annoyed and telegraphed the desire to intervene before the discomfort would dominate the brief gathering. Beer or wine and some appetizers were more the plan to relax after a thought-provoking event. He hadn't even wanted to attend such a meeting. His wife's insistence, as she always did, sometimes did pay off. Walter was getting a bit disinterested with the opening conversation. He was no dummy, but did not read as much as his wife nor have a background similar to the rest of the group. The others were on the borderline of being academics, not the elite, but folks that made their living reading and applying their knowledge on intellectual platforms. "Vera is never afraid of taking a position on opposing points of view. You guys know me -- a blue-collar servant -- and one that is content in spending time blabbering about sports, some politics and good food and wine. Golf also would help; yet, it is boring to some folks. If you guys plan to argue on the points of the speaker, I am out of here. No disrespect! It is just that my comfort zone is not in this thing. I like to win battles, too."

Fausto looked at Walter, and patted his hand. Then, with the same hand softly drumming the edge of the table, looked at him sideways and said, "Walt, I am with you. Still, we have had such a conversation every now and then. You're by far the most practical guy in this small group. Actually, in my view, that is why you are always welcomed in the conversation. Your views are simple but authentic. You could improve your golfing and your vocabulary. You are, however, like a vintage wine that one cannot separate from. We have to have it!"

Walter was acquainted with the priest's sincerity but, at times, statements with double meanings or interpretations. To Walter it could also mean some sort of cow manure. However, he respected and admired him. Actually, once one would know him well, all would come to admire him, for he was not made out of the same mold as other religious figures or servants of God. And Fausto, besides Elvera, was the only one that understood him or would realize when Walter had reached a state of boredom.

"Well ..." continued Fausto, as he understood Walter had bitten the bait. "... Max, with his own unblemished character and personality, is correct. We know where we stand on the matter of religion -- from a historical perspective and as applied in our lives in our society. The fact that he is neutral even makes his points more interesting."

Everyone, including Max, remained attentive. Respect for Father Fausto Mancini was also vintage. Being a religious man and an agent of spiritual wisdom, all also knew he was no ordinary Roman Catholic priest. He was an ordinary human being as opposed to a preacher and pontificator. As he spoke, others listened. Even Walter and Herbert, the Lutheran minister, gave notice they were game with whatever Fausto would say.

"I guess Vera's opening was pointed to a specific subject that we, at best, find it superficially familiar. You know, in pure and typical terms, Atheism is not an everyday subject of discussion. I guess she does not intend it to occupy our entire time. Instead, I suspect she means to have a casual chat while we enjoy our drinks." Fausto saw smiles of approval. Then proceeded: "Suppose we agree to a few exchanges on the matter. Just a few."

They voiced no reply. Instead, they concentrated on the drinks the waiter had just dropped off at their table. Wine for Elvera, Herbert and Max; and Heineken beer for Walter and Fausto. The garlic bread, fried calamari rings, and fried zucchini did generate eye-wows from the group.

Max, being the reluctant argument participant rushed with his answer: "I can handle a few exchanges now, assuming we will join the project. Besides I don't think the project will be about the importance and the actual perceived growth of Atheism. It is a too narrow subject to be discussed by obvious dissenters. That is my take."

"I agree with Max -- we can have just a warm up now and nothing else," injected Herbert. "Can we do that? What do you say, Vera?"

"Great, no problem. I started by citing that opening statement only to validate the speaker's point and need for our participation or the three hundred or so that were at that conference. The man with a PhD degree in theology and philosophy was just one of a few professors trying to experiment with something different. Yet, his emphasis was on Atheism -- plain and simple. Not in theoretical terms; but in practical living experiences.

"Are you sure it is all about Atheism?" asked Max.

"Of course, I am not sure until the pertinent details are known. It could be a noble project where we could use our honesty to also make some points; at least points on the intended students. But to me it could be a trap."

Elvera continued with the same noted enthusiasm and inspiration. "For me to separate what I believe and sometimes preach is a challenge that I am not too sure I can handle. Providing my views on a matter like that is asking too much. Life without God is a condition I never thought about. I could not believe being without that comfort. However, his appeal was valid. It is only a study. Still it provides comfort and justification for the atheistic society and way of life. The only thing we need to agree upon now is to be part of the project or give a pass. It is still months away for a decision that is still short of additional details and timelines."

"Funny and well put, Vera. In this case, we can put some thoughts together. I know the Atheism environment better than all of you. Not to boast anything about my family ties; just to surrender to non-bias discussion." Max was politely convincing.

All agreed as they were aware of Max's background and the history of his grandfather's fervent alliances with Atheism and in some measure with the Marxist doctrine. The fact that Max's father was a mild agnostic, and Max a militant one, took nothing away from what Max delivered in life or at the present time what Max represented to all in the group, to their organization and to the society in general. Max was a vivid example of someone who, by his versatility on all religions and creeds but maintaining a neutral behavior, represented the best and the most believable way of living life on our planet. Respect came to him almost instantaneously. He was so gifted, that people paid attention to his opinions and points of view.

"Well Max, I think we do not need to go there, or add any pertinent discussion on the initial professor's statement. We had agreed to attend this short conference, out of curiosity, for the topic was challenging. If we collectively agree to participate in one of the projects is another story. And, if we participate, we will, by the inherent and implied responsibility expose our views on this critical matter," added Elvera.

The others were not buying Elvera's stand now. They felt she was tiptoeing or withdrawing from any discussion. "Wait guys. I do not mind sharing a bit of my peace. However, in the end, I suspect that the materials will, by the mission of the project, give nothing but credibility to Atheism in its practical form. You can be good and do good without being spiritual, without taking into account what stirs in my heart and soul."

Elvera was not floundering; yet, she was giving notice that Atheism's practicality was no match to the colors, sounds, the flavors of the inner battles within one's soul. They, by knowing Elvera well, could interpret that Atheism had no soul, no color. As it was inherently insipid and mathematically predictable. "Wait, wait, again. I am kind of hurting Max's feelings. It is the furthest from my mind." She reached for Max's right shoulder. Not content, she almost dropped her head on his shoulder. Walter smiled, Max was perplexed and speechless. "Max does not espouse Atheism, much less any Marxist doctrine. He, himself, unofficially disavowed his grandfather's doctrine, in spite of loving him dearly. But, in practical terms, pure Atheism and Marxism are devoid of pure love, pure meditative circumstances and feelings. They're combative towards the introspective moments in one's life or are the reason for doing things beyond the black and white. Max speaks for himself by his behavior."

"Thanks, Vera, for the touch of affection. I too have learned a lot from you. By saying this with respect and this way is like transmitting my intolerance of Marxism and Atheism. I was present on the last moments of my dad's life. I still can go back to the time of the last few words we exchanged. Those moments sustain me. My grandfather was a different story. I have no idea what he felt in his last drops of life, vitality and elucidative spins. I cannot even suspect if there were some modifications at all. Granted he was milder and more pensive at the end of his journey. However, he never gave me a clue as to where he stood then. Perhaps he believed I read something in his behavior. He trusted my instincts. Four hours before he passed away, his motionless face, naked of any signs of life, could not communicate anything. And, that's too bad. I could not compare his dying moments with the ones I had observed with my father. Of course, my uncle's moments were shared and transmitted by my cousins."

Inside Herbert's head a light bulb lit and the others noticed by his half-raised hand and broad smile. "We can tame our discussion and focus on a collective understanding of our mission or desire to participate in the project. At the same time, we can become relevant and neutral on what we believe. Max has a pass on the subject matter. However, he's equally challenged. His religious or neutrality in any aspect of religious forces or atheistic grounds is no picnic. What I suggest now is to enjoy our drinks and food and agree to coming up with an idea to also include Sam in the project. Not his life per say; but we can use his example as a fundamental conclusion that one does not need to brag about the religious powerhouses' claim or the stake on social needs and assistance. Sam, by his homelessness and practical activism, is the perfect and neutral example. If we concentrate on his deeds," now finishing and smirking meekly, "we could be genius."

"You guys still do not know the rules of the game. Much discussion without these rules and parameters is like paying interest ahead of the due date," said Walter with a funny tone.

"Look who is talking, the wise man," said Elvera, fetching for her purse, as if meaning to leave.

"That's the way I see your intentions, like having made a commitment without knowing the rules. Anyway, thanks guys. I am ordering another beer. Any takers? More wine Max; Vera? And you Fausto, one more for the road?" Walter was happy that the gathering could be directed to different matters. Some of the intellectual stuff the others were volleying back and forth could be beyond his league.

"Not me, Walt," said Fausto. "Nothing for the road. The cops will not forgive me -- a priest much less."

"Certainly, they should not. By profession you drink every day," added Herbert.

"That was below the belt," retorted Fausto. He patted Herbert's elbow. The others also took a pass on additional drinks. Walter did not blink. In the face of the others objections, he asked the waiter for the bill instead.

"That was a good example, Herb. Sam is the perfect example. Indeed, the only valid example; even if we suspect his heart and soul are in constant action."

"I respect the opinion. Although I cannot put my finger on what he thinks and believes. What I know is that he is a gem of a human being, and a helping machine in action," concluded Max.

"Are we talking about Sam now?" asked Walter.

"No, let's adjourn with a good taste in our mouths." offered Elvera.

Elvera

A conversation with God

----

*"A word or a smile is often enough
to put fresh life in a despondent soul."*
----- *St. Therese of Lisieux*

She woke up, looked around. Her room seemed the same as ever or as the night before; just that the sunlight had invaded her space. *What a bright morning ahead,* she thought.

What a dream — fascinating and riveting -- she then mumbled to herself. Father Anthony de Mello, yes, that Jesuit priest was also in the mix. But that was long ago, twenty years ago for sure. She had read some of his books then. And also read a couple of books from Lee Strobel, the journalist turned preacher or perhaps philosopher. One book was read very recently; the other was a few years back.

Elvera got up, took a lukewarm shower. She felt good and invigorated. The body felt relaxed, clean; her mind was not. Her mind was busy for this time of the day; it was active -- tracing back the dream. The brain, like her body, was not dirty. However, she needed more than a lukewarm mind bath to shake and sort off the many images she still possessed of the dream. Perhaps a cold shower would do better. With her feet protected by a pair of slippers that were cold seconds before and then turned warm by the heat of her own feet, she marveled at this simple but scientifically possible reality: feet warm in bed, slipped in cold slippers and then now both warm again. She thought: great analogy in relationship — offer warmth and warmth will return to you. *Is this God still talking to me? Wow, I can't believe this thing.*

Anyway, Elvera, not disturbed but now certainly more confused, left her bedroom, veered to the corridor and in the direction of the kitchen. The dream was not helping the routine management of her typical day. Granted that nowadays her days looked the same -- all Saturdays, interrupted by a solitary Sunday. She had, at the pleading of her husband, retired earlier than usual. Either way, her days were different than when she had a real job. Still, busy days. "What shall I eat?" she asked herself. "I can't decide."

"Oh, Lord, my breakfast time is the easiest of my daily tasks." Indeed, it was the most joyful portion of her day; the least complicated. Elvera always kept a simple routine of varied breakfast choices. Cereal, yogurt and tea three times a week; a toasted English muffin with cream cheese, jelly and fruit and tea -- twice a week; once a week a strip of bacon, heated in the microwave, with two soft-boiled eggs and a slice of all grain wheat bread. The unplanned once a week was her choice to be surprised when she joined her friends for breakfast after the weekly morning Mass. Waffles or pancakes at the local family restaurant were more often than not the surprise. She wished an *IHop* restaurant would be nearby. No, she would not do that, for even while she worked, she rarely ate alone.

Finally, still struggling and tossing out her thoughts and plans, she made a decision; one that offered the least resistance. She poured some water in the kettle and turned the electrical power setting to on -- boiling mode. She grabbed a tea mug and let a tea bag find the bottom ensuring the bag tag held by the tiny string stayed up and girded the outside of the cup. Stubbornly, as she poured the hot, scalding water in the mug, the whole thing -- the tea bag with string and label -- fell in; just as in a Red Bull diving contest. With the help of the teaspoon, she carefully pulled it out and repositioned it as she thought it should be.

Elvera gently immersed the bag down and then up and down again a few more times until the colorless and transparent water gave way to a caramel type color -- perhaps a deep amber color. The tea bag was pulled out, set aside and assigned to replicate its mission of another cup of tea drunk at snack time. The marriage of the scalding water with the infusion of herbal tea aromas not only produced swirling vapor but also a soothing effect. She was happy and now relaxed. Elvera could not recognize with certainty the type of herbal tea flavor the packet contained. After the first sip, the taste revealed it was spicy, mint flavored. As the vapor swirls continued and found space in her nostrils, curiosity took over the need to know. She checked the tea packet wrapping -- a gourmet type -- most likely brought from one of the hotels she had stayed in a few weeks back. All of these, as well as "one cup" coffee packets, and some of the ubiquitous tiny bath bottles would conveniently find room in her carry-on luggage. As was her habit, Elvera would not open them, for she would bring her own shampoo, body lotion and sometimes special soaps. Yet, she would gladly save the hotels' typical bath items for later on sharing them with her grandkids. Their school traditionally asked for such and other items usually discarded, for acts of charity school projects. The cereal, cooked in the microwave, was done. Cereal, yogurt and tea were set on the kitchen table. The three would be companions for a few warm morning minutes.

Oh, she forgot something so crucial. How could she have forgotten her medicine: two pills -- iron and supplements -- for the morning, and the remaining three before bedtime. The medicine organizer was one of those inventions she did not have to invent herself. She thanked the organizer and whoever had invented it, for she had forgotten what day of the week it was. *Is today Thursday? Hah, thank you organizer for confirming it.* Indeed, it was -- the slot was still full with the yet to be taken medicine of five pills of distinct sizes and colors.

The dream details came back. She forced herself to revisit all of them, even the small ones, and attempt to save them in her brain. And possibly take notes. Certainly, this was not a run-of-the-mill dream thing. It had power; and therefore, it should also have significant meaning. Such as requiring consultation with the so-called dream interpretation experts, like her church pastor.

Elvera quickly remembered that throughout the Bible -- Old and New Testaments -- dreams were the most utilized means of receiving communication from the Almighty. The dream, from the Gospel of Matthew, which Elvera remembered more than any other, was the one that Joseph received -- "get up, take Mary and the baby and depart for Egypt. Herod plans to kill the baby, the Messiah." Elvera knew that the dream's message was much longer than that simple phrase. But for the moment it was good enough to render credibility to her own dream. She also remembered that Joseph suspected the baby was destined to stir things up in the world. Later on, the baby, the trouble-maker and savior of humanity, would attract fishermen of souls, confound the elite, the academic, and then, at the end of His journey, cause some uncertainty on his followers. "He is no longer with us. What do we do now? He had an ignominious type of death, and was defeated; or will he come back as the real king or the real shepherd? Will he?"

That was what Elvera thought the apostles and disciples must have conjured and felt at that time. Instead, she ventured imagining on what Joseph would have thought later. "Will this baby be part of God's conspiracy to teach His stubborn people a lesson?"

A lesson that Joseph was unaware of or could not predict the outcome of the child he was ordained to teach some rudimental carpenter's skills? Or how to function with his friends in his early years? The baby, now a teenager, lecturing in the temple? To the Elite? "Isn't this the son of the carpenter? From Nazareth? What good comes from Nazareth, a town of no consequence?" Joseph kept his silence, in compliance with prophesies. "What do I know but rationalize that prophesies must be fulfilled; the dots must be connected. After all, the Book says I am the one to maintain the lineage -- from David to me and then, by association, I am the father of Jesus. For my wife was chosen among all women to bear that savior of the world. I know I am just a carpenter. But with a role to which no one else was assigned and entrusted. Here we go – it thus follows that the Almighty made a simple carpenter important; like the humble shall inherit the Kingdom of God."

Elvera chuckled with smiles and thoughts of the folk language that swirled in her head. She felt good and then fetched for a paper notebook and meant to take some notes -- legible bullet point notes. *I have to take notes before the details of the dream fade away. These dreams are like poetry with some sounds of music. Indeed, I must take notes, for my brain at times is lazy or stubborn in saving and then revealing great memories.*

∞∞∞∞∞

Elvera was relieved she had overcome the dream; the folk talk she had with herself in the morning and the decision to reveal it to Walter before she would avail herself of any dream interpretation experts. Actually, the only expert she had in mind was her Church pastor Father Richard Lukas. She knew he was good, always well prepared for his homilies, and also very diligent in getting the parishioners involved in all aspects of the parish life. But there was a little drawback. He was or always seemed eternally busy. Choosing the confessionary for a long dialogue would not be fair because sometimes or at certain times of the year lines would form for confession. She thought that, with good notes duly recorded, the dream would not go away. Instead, she felt that talking with her husband first would be a good idea. Now, that she was retired and Walter just visited the shop for a few hours a day, both had more time to chat. Walter was a good listener; she would claim to friends. Besides, she felt that both were growing in love with each other. Contrary to lives of other couples fully engaged in professional careers, where now retirement and "twenty-four-seven" free days meant competing for space, and some bickering of sorts, their more frequent presence on a daily basis was unequivocally a blessing. Not a pretense, but a blessing, period. Elvera and Walter relished their presence with open arms. The fact that both had different temperaments, enduring mutual respect, a respect for their own pursuits of time management, enabled them to view their closeness as a gift rather than an intrusion. She would wait for Walter, or until he returned from his once a week golf game.

∞∞∞∞∞

Oh, she remembered that day that clicked with a soft curiosity and then with a "bang -- this is it; we are in love and thus must find lasting togetherness." It was a wedding event that put them face to face, drink to drink and dance to dance almost all night. Not really. They thought they could, but it was not their wedding. The bridegroom was Walter's cousin and the bride was Elvera's work mate. Both were in the wedding party and Walter was the best man. During the wedding's rehearsal session and later on the customary dinner, Walter and Elvera came to trade some smiles, know their names and the reason they had been chosen to escort the soon-to-be new couple. That spark that could ignite a romance was not felt then or the spark plug was still wrapped in its box, a little distance away from doing its job of igniting an engine to full life.

"Walt or Walter? I heard both."

"My real name is Walter. However, everybody calls me Walt." He paused, then resumed as Elvera thought he had more to add. "I heard yours is Vera. Right?"

"Like you, I have a real name and the short name. And like you, both are soft abbreviations. Elvera is my birth name and the name that my mother used to call when she was mad at me. I like Elvera and Vera at the same time. Makes no difference."

"Then we shall call you Vera. Unless, I guess, I get mad at you."

Elvera chuckled while still holding her champagne glass, almost spilling it over her lap, to the garden grounds. Walter held her hand, she flushed and then recomposed herself. "Sorry, but I did not expect your statement." Walter smiled too, offered his own cocktail napkin so that Elvera would clean her glass while holding her hand and a portion of her dress.

"I don't know what got into me to repeat your mother's sweet reprimand. It just came out. I could perhaps mimic your mother raising her voice... 'Eelllvera!!!'"

"You are funny. I like your posture." Trying to change the theme of the conversation, Elvera turned her attention to the wedding itself. "This has been a great wedding. Everybody is happy and the messages offered to the bride and groom were terrific. I like yours about your cousin, how you guys were always in trouble and that your father was stern to both of you. Your backgrounds are also interesting -- very interesting!" Elvera stopped while Walter kept gazing at her, almost causing a little discomfort. In good faith, Walter was enjoying her narrative, adding his interest beyond her eyes; actually, through her eyes. "Well, just the places that my ancestors came from. Different countries but yet so close." She stopped. Walter took over. He had to. Otherwise, he would make Elvera more uncomfortable. Both sipped more champagne, were served more as waiters could find the garden grounds and refresh the guests with more of the sparkling juice.

"I was not that good in school but remember my geography classes. There is such a thing as Basque countries -- the Spanish and the French. That is also when history needs to be linked to geography. And they are rewriting themselves in changes after changes." Elvera waited because, with very little living experience, she too was curious about where she had come from. This apparent solemn direction of conversation was now putting her at ease -- a different and welcome feeling.

In less than ten minutes, Elvera learned that Walter was born in Modesto, moved with his parents and sister to Castro Valley, completed High School, reluctantly did odd jobs at his father's shop as a self-employed heating and air conditioning business, rarely got along well with him, due to not only generational and background differences, but also differences in temperament. Enlisting in the Navy and then changing to the Coast Guard service, allowed Walter to hone his independence, grow in personality, ambition and regrets. Regrets because he blamed himself, his immaturity for not having enjoyed his father's company as a good, obedient son should. He knew he was not the cause of his dad's death, but also knew that things could have been different. Granted that his father was stern, demanding and at times isolated. He was dying and Walter did not know it. Walter, in spite of recognizing his father's at times unnecessary stern approach, later on regretted and placed the finger on himself solely because he had more advantages in life unlike his father's life and upbringing back in France. There, in a small village not too far from Biarritz, France's deep southwest, life was harsh. His father could have shared some details and so could his mother. But pride and old country's culture were in the way of some sort of reconciliation. Certainly, Walter came to recognize his father's aloofness a little late, too. He made amends and Elvera filled the voids later. For he would love her forever.

"That is a very neat story. Indeed, immigrants always have great stories to tell and they are always surrounded by drama. Now, you mentioned Biarritz, where your ancestors came from. I know this resort town. On one of the few trips my parents took me, we stayed there on the way to Lourdes."

"Me too. I made a pilgrimage to Santiago de Compostela."

"Really? But Santiago is on the west side of Spain!"

"You're right. However, besides wanting to find my roots, I wanted to cleanse my doubts about life after my father passed away.

31

In reality, I could not focus on what I needed to do. I left my father's small business in the hands of the only other worker he had. He was a good technician, too. Thus, I departed for a long journey that lasted almost three months."

"How sweet and brave."

"Yes, sweet it was. Brave I don't know about that. Although the major Pilgrimage starts in France, less than thirty miles from Spain, I took different routes. I started in Biarritz, walked westbound via San Sebastian, along the coastline until I crossed down towards the French way." Noticing some confusion in Elvera's look, Walter clarified "there are several major routes to Santiago. The most popular or most walked is the French Way. However, I had no particular timeline to follow. I drifted via several Caminos and then caught the Camino Francês."

"See, you shared courageous odysseys. You also said you walked. That means you carried a back pack and slept under the stars!"

"Yes, a few days under the stars, but mostly in hostels and a few stays in small inns."

"Again, I think what you did is or was fascinating and brave."

"Thanks. Let's talk about you instead. I innocently added some drama. Your past must be full of cheers." Elvera remained silent, pensive. Walter recharged. "Cheers, one more sip. Life is good to me. I still have a mom alive."

Elvera slowly raised her glass towards Walter's glass and found courage to tell her story. Moments before they had agreed to take a walk in the hotel's garden, Elvera had casually introduced her parents to Walter. The introductions were so casual and on the borderline of an awkward event.

"My story has two phases -- the very sad and the happy one. I am living the happy one. Yet, sometimes looking back at what happened that I don't fully know and what could have happened, makes me wonder about God's plans. Two wonderful Good Samaritans coming to my life had to be a God's gift. A miracle for sure."

She stopped as she noticed Walter's eyes welling up a bit but displaying, what for her, were attentive eyes. She continued. "I just cannot explain any other way. For instance, the couple I clumsily introduced as my parents are the Good Samaritans -- my adoptive parents." Walter pursed his lips; and timidly waived his right hand for Elvera to proceed. "I never knew my father and barely knew my mother. She died only six years after my birth." Walter wanted her to continue but feared the outcome would become a little heavy. After all he was at a wedding gathering, was finding love beyond other experiences he had had before; perhaps he did not want to learn it all this moment. Elvera continued as she attempted not to look directly at Walter's eyes; instead, looked downward, almost sideways -- deliberately.

"But you said you were also Basque; from the Spanish side," Walter reluctantly added.

"I did? Well, let me then fill the blank spots." Walter observed that Elvera used smart analogies with ease. "My adoptive father, a product prospector, used to go to Spain every year during the harvesting of grapes and olives season. Barcelona was his destination. A few months before I was born, my adoptive parents, after the usual business trip, extended their stay towards a deserving vacation. San Sebastian, a beautiful city on the coastline, was the destination. It was my luck, for during their stay they met my birth mother; pregnant with me. But also, with a very sad story."

"How come?" Elvera stopped and did not mind the unnecessarily-timed interruption. "I am sorry. I love what you are narrating, it is so romantically sad. Yet, let's find a spot at the bar instead. What do you say?"

"Okay, we can do that. Meantime let me warn my parents that I found romance and that they can go home by themselves." It was time for Walter to chuckle and reduce his melancholy. He did, lost his voice, helped Elvera up, joined her until she located her parents. From a distance Walter waived back at her parents, waited for Elvera, and found good space in the bar.

"Where were we?" questioned Elvera.

"Not yet. Let's have a drink first. No more champagne."

"No more alcohol for me. I'll take ginger ale on the rocks. I will wait and retrace my thoughts while you fetch the drinks. And with less detail and drama." Walter smiled.

"You still need help for where we were?"

Elvera offered a "nah..." voice and hand gesture. "My mother was a maid at the resort my adoptive parents stayed. She also was taking refuge at a Catholic Sisters' house. She had no husband and no relatives to speak of. My birth father as well as my grandfather and my mother's two brothers were gunned down by Franco's fascist soldiers during the Spanish Civil war. Terrible! Just as Mussolini did to his brothers and sisters during World War II -- kill at will." Walter was taking a mental note for even if the terminology -- places, persons and time -- were not foreign to him, the details were. "And just for the reason that they were poor and thus resembling the opposition party." She paused again and then Walter recognized that the docile lady also possessed some social pup, some inner courage. "My adoptive parents became interested in my mom's plight and voiced the desire to adopt me once I would come to exist. They met the sisters who willingly offered to help with the arrangements of adoption and beyond."

"Are you okay that I proceed?" Walter nodded a yes. "I will not detail much more, but need to put an end to this saga, the final points." She drank of her drink and proceeded. "My parents, now possessing the necessary adoption details, flew to San Sebastian, became my parents. Adoptive, of course."

"Great story. And then?"

"Well, once this is known there is not much more to tell other than my mother passed away a few years later. More precisely when I was five years old and after I, with my adoptive parents, visited her for the first time."

"This is good material for a movie. You have saints for adoptive parents. What a story!"

"You are right. My parents are living angels, a living proof that God thinks of everybody. Look at this..." she continued "... not only did they offer me a life my mother could not provide, but also helped her with money as well as money for the Sisters' house. Every year since my adoption. Listen to this ..." Elvera took a brief break while Walter stayed in suspense "... My parents told the sisters that in the event my mother wanted to take me back, they would do that. Of course, they would prefer that my mother never thought of that possibility. As a childless couple, they wanted me so badly, they've loved me unconditionally and have lasted long enough to see me represent them well; and make them proud of their decision. God bless them."

"Wow. What a background to share with others of family interest. Thanks for sharing. I would be honored to meet you again. Can we do that?"

"Of course; I enjoyed talking with you. Besides I can't remember sharing my life with others like I did with you. A dinner with the newlyweds could help."

"Do we have to wait for that chance --- newlyweds? Unless you are engaged."

Elvera laughed softly, more like a fastidious smile, then said: "Engaged! Are you serious or making a random statement? I don't remember catching that bouquet of flowers the bride threw up in the air. Did you see that?"

"You're right and funny. Engagement was not the right word."

"Don't worry Walt. Can I call you Walt?" Walter nodded yes. "You see, let me tell my age. A mistake that women commit and should avoid. I am twenty-eight but very busy with my work; my bosses depend on me. My parents also depend on me. Remember they were in their mid- forties when I was adopted. They do not need any caregivers help; yet, I mean a lot to them. Then I am busy with some civic endeavors, including those at my own parish. See ... I have no time for engagements. Unless..."

Walter stopped her in her tracts. Being that Elvera was being brave, he willed not to take a secondary role. "Unless, what? Does it mean we can have a date?"

"Why not? I have time to date you and figure out if you are real; I have no hidden commitments. At least I know your ancestors are from the Basque region. The rest I can take care of myself. Yes. When?"

Walter's romantic and thus far measured approach, instantaneously became no match to Elvera's bold command of the conversation. Unprepared, he blushed and admitted to himself that, Elvera's turn-around posture also offered enormous pleasant possibilities. They traded telephone numbers, certain potential dates and gentle hugs.

That recollection was so sweet. Not better than the dream. But immensely sweet. Walt is the love of my life, my companion conceived in heaven but very alive on earth. I will wait for him. I must chat about the dream. At least to get a good start.

She finished the tea and would go for a walk to breathe some necessary fresh air and improve the recollection of the dream's details. Walter would help. After all he was so practical, so authentic.

∞∞∞∞∞

"I am glad you are home. You're late or later than usual. That means you must have played eighteen holes. Anything else interesting?"

Walter kissed Elvera on the cheeks as usual. But noticed her eyes brilliantly mischievous. "You are smiling so broadly. What's new? What's in the news? Any calls from your children with the usual surprises? Which happen frequently!"

"The same old same. I am tired of politics. They are making me sick. I've got to turn the TV off and cell phone as well. But I got a call from Karen. She says you guys landed a job from a good builder. I guess you knew that."

"Don't tell me ... was it from B&N Development? They did?"

"Yup, they did. All of their sixteen custom homes. And with no changes and price adjustments."

"Well, it is time to celebrate. That will require we hire more technicians. Can we celebrate now? Go out for some grub?"

"No. I cooked the usual easy way -- beef stroganoff. It came out good. I am honing my culinary skills. Even average meals now come out gourmet. Maybe we can go out tomorrow."

Walter reached for Elvera, hugged her profusely, adding kisses she loved so tenderly. "Listen, it is nothing about the business and the fact we landed a good job. It is about you. I am so lucky to have you in my life. God may demand more from me as a pay back of sorts. Let's have our stroganoff and talk about the weekend, starting tomorrow."

"Great idea. And what you said is true. God may demand more from us for giving us too many good things. We must pay back with no short cuts. We must."

"I will go to the shop tomorrow morning to check on the contract. Then, let's get the suitcases ready for a weekend in Monterey. We'll leave tomorrow, early afternoon and think about how to pay God back."

While having their supper, Elvera, besides trading news on the kids and grandkids, approached Walter on the dream she had. As the narration took the usual start, Walter offered an alternative. "Vera, the way you feel so strong and emotional about this dream, can we wait for tomorrow? Can you retain the details? Even the ones with juices and quirks? I had a good game, came across a new player for our group and found him to be a gem of a human being. This meal is delicious. Let's wrap the night up with a movie. What do you say? Can we do that?"

"On the big screen?! Yes, we can and should. No, I will not forget the details, I took notes."

Walter smiled, reached for her again with another hug. "I am lucky to have you. I can't forget you retiring early with still energy to spare. Giving up a career that meant a lot to you and our family. You were the bread earner for a long time. This takes guts. I hope you are happy you did what others resent doing so early."

"Walt, you are right but we need to correct your thinking. Yes, as a Northern California executive, the job paid well, very well. My bosses appreciated my dedication and the results I added to the whole. However, nothing is forever. Nothing but you, our family and our community, can be traded for a job and position. Prestige is just in people's minds, short duration and ego. It takes you nowhere or near the things of our heart and soul. Besides I was not delivering real value to the community needs. Now I have more time." Walter's attention was revealing the same attention he paid her on that first romantic conversation of thirty-four years earlier. "Now we can pay God back more measurably. That is what you said minutes ago."

"Let's see the movie."

3

Elvera

A conversation with God --- sequel

"Heaven is filled with converted sinners of all kinds, and there is room for more."
----- *St. Joseph Cafasso*

Afterall we did not talk about the dream on Friday. Although we left Castro Valley early, early enough to be in our summer home before five, the traffic was horrible. We had only time to drop our stuff in the house and then find a place to eat. There was also no need to search for anything fancy. The usual hole-in-the-wall restaurant always served us well; the owners knew us and we were always satisfied eating there.

That said, we postponed the sharing and eventual deep discussion of the dream for Saturday. Or so we thought. It did not happen either for Walter had a list of small projects in our home in Monterey. It is just a sixteen hundred square foot home requiring less than five minutes of walking to reach the ocean. It has one large master bedroom, two small bedrooms, two bathrooms, and a detached car garage. Although we could afford to make large and convenient improvements, like adding more space and modern stuff, we opted to stay put. Even now, because we never thought of having homes to look like museums and/or have state-of-the-art conveniences. The big cottage was good enough for us and for our three children and their brood whenever time permitted them to visit it. Kids, in many sports activities with games and tournaments on weekends, denied them the pleasures of the ocean and beach environments. For that reason and others, we never had there, the whole family together. Besides, we love our Bay Area, particularly on the East side with easy access to three major highways. We thought we were blessed with unique and old fashion neighborhoods, and were close to the best of the Bay. Indeed, we would brag to friends from other places that the Bay Area, with its diversity, was as unique as one group of seven million people could be. An expensive living for some, but a reliable area where reliability was entrusted to decent civic leaders.

Therefore, we let the Saturday be a Saturday -- relaxation without exploring some new cooking adventures. These types of cooking relaxation and joys were then relegated to more revolutionary ways of physical, mental and spiritual expeditions; such as walking on the beach and using the iconic trails. Walter was not an avid walker. He preferred long but leisure walking where he and I would feel free to air out all of our many thoughts and sometimes intimate emotions. Not guarded and polished, but just free riding exchanges. The past was not that much revisited. It was like the immediate past that included our recent decisions to modify our impact on careers, and the challenges that our children and now growing grandchildren were facing in their lives. These mattered. The status of the world where more bad news obliterated the news that could earn the coveted prize that the *glass was half full* also mattered. Many times, we laughed that some of the bad news derived from decisions that we had not approved. The variables were so many that juxta-positioning them would cause civil wars.

On the cooking side, for certain, I was never known for being a gourmet chef or a pioneer in the nouveau culinary expeditions. Yet, my cooking never embarrassed me. I held my ground on typical family food on weekdays and expanded to weekend creative meals. Watching and learning from my mother-in-law, I could replicate her skill and cook great Basque food or food borrowed from the other regions -- like Paella from Galicia. And that was exactly what I cooked for the Saturday -- Paella Louisiana style. Walter even used to say in my early years watching and taking notes from my mother-in-law's old fashion and flavorful cooking that: *you honor my mother with your "from the old country's cuisine."* Indeed, I learned from her how to cook Paella, Octopus salad, or served whole with the body and the tentacles spread on a wood serving board. But, above all, I learned to choose and bake good lamb chops.

∞∞∞∞∞

"Are you ready? Really?"

"Darn! After too many false starts, I have to be ready. I am actually better prepared to start the recollection. I improved my notes to confirm the details are secure, real and reflect our values."

I was ready and Walt was serious; for, like me, wanting to share, he wanted to listen. It involved matters dear to both of us. Walt rarely read the Bible on purpose; it was not his thing. He read articles, short dissertations on matters of the Gospels, the church's bulletin and other material I suggested he read. I actually felt comfortable with the way he managed his spirituality -- practical and to himself. It was far better than mine. While he took our faith as it was without any special emotional stress, I had to dig for more proof of anything; I had to invest some inner acceptance of the occult. There was some innocence in Walt's practical ways, but he had an unequivocal approach to matters dear to his heart. Walt always extended a hand to anyone who genuinely asked for help. His employees were the first to get the feel and smell of all he was about. But if you crossed him, he would let you know that the one who lost was the one who received. He used to say: "I never regret what I do for others; I feel sorry for those who betray the good hand when extended -- the gesture of the Good Samaritan."

After Sunday Mass, when in Monterey, we went for our typical brunch, and then back to our living room for some TV viewing and reading. Our living room, more like a family room (one we did not have), was a favorite place to spend a placid Sunday afternoon. With no obligations of any kind, Walter had decided we would return to Castro Valley on Monday. No TV viewing -- our Raiders were not playing in this time slot. With no reading, we were ready!

"Okay, we are ready. But let's have a brief discussion on dreams. Let's talk about what we remember and what we have learned." As usual, me, the college graduate girl initiated the drill. "Do you know how long they last, what matters or events they deal with, or where they happen?"

"I never read anything about dreams or how they happen or their length. We talk, forget, and move on."

"Good point" I said. "And I bet yours would be different from mine. You may take your responsibilities with a high degree of seriousness, but never fanatically or pushing yourself to the limits.

You know me -- I am different. So, my dreams reflect my busy mind."
As usual, Elvera was pontificating like an expert on dreams.

"Okay, nice. How long do they last?" demanded Walter.

"They can last a few seconds, on an average, or as long as thirty minutes."

"That long?"

"Like I said -- yours, by your very personality and temperament, should not last long. That is the way you are -- simple, effective and uncomplicated. They should not last long."

"You are being nice to me. Any plans for the rest of the day? Shall we rent a room?"

"See, you are funny. I am also funny but you are seriously and intelligently funny. Thanks. As for renting a room, we shall see." Elvera extended her hand to Walter. He kissed her instead.

"Okay, professor -- start the story."

∞∞∞∞∞

"I entered a place that, to me, did not look like heaven. I went through a glass door, or so it seemed, and encountered nothing but people being escorted towards a reception area. I followed the crowd and came to this enormous half-moon reception area. There, receptionists working on computers, either interrogated people or dispatched them to ushers who escorted them to designated areas. Everything was displayed on the big screens that covered the wall -- whatever looked like walls. There were no names, background, hobbies, deeds, misdeeds, no ages, no places of origin, gender distinctions and other personal attributes. No pictures, nothing."

In this big hall, there were six gates, the size of rolling door gates in large warehouses, just like the one on your shop. Two gates on each side -- in front of us, two to the right side and two to the left." Elvera paused for a moment, seeing no signs of Walter holding back but giggling; nevertheless, she felt comfortable in proceeding. "I am glad you're not laughing." Walter waved her to continue. "Each gate had a color that kind of matched the colors of the incoming traffic and which glowed on their wrists. Mine was yellow. I looked at my wrists and they glowed yellow, in a bracelet type glow. The other colors, as I noticed later on, were, let me see, green, black, blue and grey. I am missing one color. I remember ... that's it ... orange. Orange! Certainly, this color was next to my gate."

"No white door gates?"

"Nope. The only white I saw was the white of the ushers, like angel white. No wings. But they, hundreds I presume, moved so effortlessly, like skating without skates. Everything on their part floated."

"So, the color on your wrists matched the color of your gate. Meaning you belonged to the yellow section. Could you tell the number of people in each section? Did some or other wrists display more colors than other gates?"

"Can't remember. I did not take notes of that. Unless, let me think ... yes, 'green; had less people. And that was when I signaled for one usher to explain the significance of colors."

"And..."

"I became disappointed. Yellow, meant I had to wait long for a meeting with the Lord or assistants."

"Or Saint Peter," Walter retorted while cracking up with laughter.

"What's so funny? Of course, I was disappointed in waiting too long."

"That was a dream. Why getting so sad?"

Elvera, now comforted with Walter's mild and ironic interjection, proceeded in building her narrative before she met with God. She recounted with vivid pleasure, entrants immediately marked with white, being escorted behind the reception area and never seen again. These were young people, dressed normally, humbly and others in rags, with scars from wounds inflicted perhaps in slums anywhere in the world, with t-shirts framed with pictures and descriptions in different languages. A few older people also possessed white bracelets. She guessed these people were going directly to heaven.

Then she directed her narrative to those supposedly marked red. These, coming on a rolling carpet, bypassed everything. No descriptions of names, name to fame misdeeds or crimes were seen. They all came in attire as perhaps as they had died -- three-piece suits, cocktail gowns, bikinis, swim shorts, deck shoes and nightgowns. Their faces showed disgusting or horrific glares. During the long wait, Elvera could surmise that as they arrived through the revolving door, and once they had glanced down to their right, they must have felt terrorized. Others just laughed and gazed hysterically as if going to a resort or a very warm place.

"Wow. I bet they were being escorted to hell, without a chance for an interview or parole. Straight down. Or, happy with their fate."

"I guess so. Good analogy, but funny, Walt."

"You also cited the colors black and orange. And the color blue as practically going straight to heaven."

"I did. Orange was almost like yellow. Migrating to green would take longer than yellow. Black is a different story and I could not

46

grasp fully their predicament or their final destination. It encompassed people who were religious leaders of every kind, professors in religion, philosophy, theology, atheism -- you name it. I assumed it would be any professional with influence on behavior."

"Wow! That could include anybody, including priests. Unless they repented."

"I have no idea. A few of them could have belonged to any color -- including red."

"How long did you have to fulfill your job before going to the better place?"

"Looked long. But, as I was told during my interview with God, the word or meaning of time does not exist there. Nothing is measured as it is in our planet. We just feel something and then (later) try to decipher what it meant. It is just different, unexplainable. God always smiled at my questions about earthlings' habits."

Elvera resumed her story on how she meets God. Surprised in not seeing St. Peter, God tells her that the Rock is equally interviewing entrants from the colors black, grey and orange. God reserves yellow and green for Himself. She also describes the dialogues depicting her initial sadness and then the comfort in knowing that God has a role for her or all those wearing yellow. She was told that she would graduate to green in time.

"So, you talked, he interviewed you, you felt bad, then you lightened up once a role was given to you. Were you happy?"

"Of course, I was. I knew heaven would be within my reach; because God said so. It would not be a direct line, for I had more work to do. Actually, let me think how I felt. Although pride was no longer important to me, I almost felt lucky that God had a role for me -- like I was important, and had interpersonal skills." She paused, reconfigured her recollections and then said. "Walt, it is hard to describe."

"Tell it in any way you think. I am enjoying this trip of yours -- to heaven."

"How are you doing Vera? Good to see you. You've done nice work. Some more is required of you. Please, smile, for it will not last long, it will be just a little harsh at first. Smile! When you love me and your neighbor nothing is harsh! I just used the word for you to get the gist."

"Gist, like harsh -- earth's words? That is cool, God."

"Exactly. Our vocabulary is all logical and lovely. Thus, you'll be happy being useful to other candidates to heaven. It will be like pain and joy; more pain and joy and then relief that the place I prepared for you and my children will be yours forever."

"Nice to know that. Some suffering and then exhilaration. Suffering no more after my penance! Right?"

"Look at me Vera, it is like paying forward. You have done great things on earth, helped so many, you've created opportunities for my Holy Spirit to grant graces. I know, I know. You on earth think that you convert my stubborn and fallen away children. That is okay to think that way or until vanity possesses you all. I understand. I do. However, you no longer act with undue pride. You are fine. This temporary stage is … call it what you want … just a short stay before paradise. Unless many deny me, reject me, even until the last second."

"Oh, you mentioned seconds. I thought having no watches, no measuring sticks, You would not cite seconds."

"Elvera…" Elvera blinked her eyes and pursed her lips for God had addressed her earlier as Vera, an intimate approach. God resumed… "I know your mother called you Elvera when she was mad *at you. Even your husband jokes with you once in a while."* Elvera *broadened her smile. "I mentioned seconds, like in time, only to make you feel at home. I want you to feel this way -- relaxed and ready to roll up your sleeves and take on some important duties."* Elvera *was enjoying God's way of talking, his way of creating a positive environment. She also accepted God's 'Elvera' thing just as she came to accept her mother's motherly reprimand.*

"Thank you, Lord. Talking to you like this is so comfortable. Am I going to see your son? Jesus? He was my idol, my rock, my bridge to everything good."

"Not this time. He is on earth still working diligently gathering lost sheep. He, and Mother Mary are always happily rescuing lost souls or inspiring them to make amends. Always!"

"I guess everyone has a role. It is not just relaxing at the beach, or playing bridge, or playing golf with Walt. Duties!"

"Of course, there is life up here. Just immensely different from life on earth. I designed it to be like here -- a sample of paradise. But I had competition. You know that. And I had to remake the mold. Remember that in my love letter to my people?"

"You mean the Book; the Bible?"

"Good call. Good knowledge."

"You're right, God. But it was so tough to keep your commandments. We are always agitated and sometimes horrified. I am anxious coming up here, even if I am in a transition mode -- in the pipeline to heaven."

"C'mon Vera. Give me a break. I am always helping you and everyone else. The only thing you have to do is trust, trust me. Tell me the truth: when you are in touch with me, concentrating and asking for help, did I betray you? Did I leave you drifting, or did I cause you to instantly find your way to the solution for your needs?"

"No, God, never did you leave me alone when I asked for help in a sincere manner. When I was sincere in my gut, you know what I mean, I got instant help. And it feels good. You remember that; don't you? I always pleaded my pardon for not trusting you. But then when I really did, you fixed the problem, or let me fix it. And I apologized to you on my knees. Didn't I?"

"Yes, you did. Sincerity unlike repetitive prayers, not from the heart, or as you said eloquently from the gut, always got my attention. You rang the bell and I delivered."

"Lord, this is so good. Talking with you as if we were brother and sister. So cool!"

"I am glad you like it. This is the way I created you and Walter in my image. In time you will be in my place -- the place I created for you and all mankind. After all it took a great deal of thinking in creating the world with all its moving parts, and reciprocal properties, all with a variety of functions where everyone was dependent on each other. Creating you and Walter took a lot more thinking. And then my plan almost got highjacked by my right-hand angel. Jealousy, absolute jealousy. And I had to re-invent myself -- time after time. I will win until the end of time, when I will re-invent myself differently."

"Wow! Great talk. I wish I were down on earth so I could tell what I learned here. Then, with all this talk it means I am in; I am here to stay. Can I take this to the bank?"

"Funny talk, still using earth's vocabulary?"

"Well, you also used earth's lingo. So, being in, where do I go now?"

"Not too fast; let's talk about the task I have for you before you come in for good -- the eternity. The task will help me and you at the same time... C'mon ... don't make that face! Just as on earth, when faith and deeds matter, you will help me by reassuring that my children don't stray too far from my reign. Are you ready for the task?"

"But if I fail, will I still have a chance to come and stay with You? Will this take too long?"

"In earthly time it may take long. Let me tell you the details."

God explained to Elvera that her task, before coming to paradise forever, would entail following humans on earth. Staying connected through the spirit; yet, with no contacts or physical influence on the assigned human.

"Therefore, I will follow this person wherever he or she goes, have no way to make corrections on behavior, bad decisions, etc...." ... "what's there to gain, to help? Just watching bad outcomes is like torture; like purgatory!" ... "You are laughing! But I am serious! This hurts!"

"Relax Vera. The fact that there is no contact does not imply you'll have no impact. Haven't you heard of guardian angels? Haven't you heard people saying 'I was saved by a guardian angel?'"

"I guess You are right; like always. Thank you, Lord. Right now, I do not have to say 'I hope so.' Because I know so."

God smiled broadly.

∞∞∞∞∞

"Just like that! Never showing fear in talking to God. Or as if you were brothers or teammates!"

"Yes, no fear, no anguish, no second guessing, no nothing! Remember, for the last few years my approach to God and his designs has changed measurably. Sometimes I feel I am locked in with things of God. Other times, I am confused or feel lost; like God deserted me.

Or that he left me fend for myself. However, in between, I'm staying patient, accepting my sadness and my emptiness and confusion; but never wavering because I sense it is just a matter of time when I find my footing and the bridge to God. Call it the Holy Spirit, or..."

"Your ticket to heaven!" prompted Walter.

Elvera offered no rebuttal and Walter completed his thought. "Come here my love." Elvera dragged her body towards Walter and rested her head on his chest. Walter wrapped his hand around her head, her shoulders, her neck and kissed her warmly. "I would be scared of having such a dream; even if it were as sweet as what you narrated. I do not live agitated or pessimistic or concerned. We have a good life; we have a good family. Yet, once in a while I have doubts, fears or just that I am lost and far from being ready. I can't fathom life after we finish our journey. Or like you." Walter paused, thought again what to say or to direct the conversation to other matters. Then he concluded. "I have had in the past, distant past, horrible dreams, cringing dreams. Lately they are calm, almost serene. I don't know why!"

"You must have made peace with you, with your **you**. Not that you were wild or lost. I mean you got your priorities in order and created more time for serene and revealing introspection."

"We need to rent a room. Always protecting me." Elvera threw him a flirtatious smile.

Walter liked the smile but, at the moment, preferred to add one or two more questions about the dream. "What do you plan to do now with your dream? You said earlier, before choosing me for confessor, you would talk with Father Lukas. Are you going to do that?"

"I don't think so. As a parish priest, he is always busy. You know that."

"Yes, I know. Yet, he has a lot of respect for you."

"That is good. I may use other options. Still, let's be fair here. You helped me getting it out. That is more than good enough. Unless, the other members of our group find the components of the dream interesting. We'll see."

"As far as I have seen, they all admire you. Some may actually find parts of your dream as optimal discussing points. But I am not part of the group. I just join you folks for the leftovers."

"Does that bother you, Walt?"

"None whatsoever. Joining you on drinking gatherings fits me well. For instance, Father Mancini would be good. He has done it all, has been close to it all, close to dirt, to the street and to Sam. Fausto and Sam must have their own warehouse of dreams."

"Yes, Fausto would be the ideal person to share the morsels. He is on the other side of the bay. I am sure he could be conned into joining me and some others on our side; I mean Max, or even Herb. Both like good chats. Indeed, we can use the dream as an excuse to get together. I'll think about it." Elvera paused, thought more and then said: "they'll come for any excuse."

"Max would be good. Being agnostic would make more sense. He may even share his own dreams."

"Max is so authentic. A better human being than many Catholics I know. Being on the fence is not a big deal. At this time, it is more for convenience he stays agnostic. Besides, it is so soon for him to change sides. He is the president on merit and well regarded in his conference. We get along so well, though."

"What conference are you talking about? The what's it called?"

"The Agnostic Society of Northern California!" Walter was still a bit confused and she added: "Is there anyone else?"

"I had never heard of such thing. I thought you meant the one that you and Fausto, and Herb belong!" stated Walter.

"I can see the confusion for I never mentioned Max's club before. You were thinking about 'Be-a-difference-Foundation.' Two different organizations," replied Elvera.

"Then, what do we have here?" asked Walter.

"Well, Max's organization has its own mission; like a church without being a church. What do you know about the Foundation?" Inquired Elvera.

"Not much either. Just that you drag me to a function here and there, I guess and invite me to have a meal with you guys and, by default, I pay the bill," chuckled Walter.

"That is not fair. Only a couple of times and, on both occasions, you were in a Good Samaritan mood. Even my friends felt embarrassed the second time."

"Just kidding. Your friends deserve my only way to say thanks to them. It keeps me happy knowing about the people you are engaged with. I have even learned a lot with your friends. But, now, forget Max's club. How does your foundation operate? Like the Rotary?"

"No, no similarities of any kind; including the organization's structure."

"Okay, tell me more. Such as the clubs you belong, your meetings, etc." concluded Walter.

"First it is not like the Rotary or similar service clubs who have a global structure and aligned regionally, by geographic areas. *Be-a-Difference Rainbow Foundation* is philanthropic, non-sectarian organization -- created by wealthy patrons."

"Good; like "Make a Wish Foundation?" questioned Walter.

"I do not know about it; but my guess it is not like that. Leaving that notion aside, *Be-a-Difference Rainbow Foundation*, like I said, is made up of wealthy but equally very caring businessmen and businesswomen, entrepreneurs. Not on the same level as Bill Gates, Warren Buffet and the like. Our benefactors are millionaires but below billions. However, they lend their side-line energies, create support through shelters, donate their money and oversee their charity. If one wants to call it a charity, that is. They have eight councils in the Bay Area, who act as advisors on their plans and also engage in other smaller undertakings like the ones in which Fausto, Max and I are involved."

Elvera's explanation was credible; yet too vast in detail and scope. Walter's face conveyed that invitation for Elvera to convert the narrative into small change or put an end to the matter. "I suspect you are confused. It is a simple operation but far different than civic clubs. Besides the foundation moves quite a bit of money. Let me see: (1) The Foundation donates money to all deserving causes and their own cause … as I mentioned before. They have budgets, plans and receive much info on their own, for they have professional consultants; (2) aside from that, they created councils of very credentialed and good-willed volunteers. It is like me and the others you've come to know. Not only do we collect and share information, but also, on a separate level, we are assigned to evaluate such information. And, in the process, we identify individuals that reflect true and tangible **be-a-difference** human beings. This task, of selecting winners, is done once every six months.

"And that is what you and Herb and Fausto get involved…" said Walter.

"Exactly! For instance, I do belong to the Advisory Board -- that big money part -- and also to one of the eight councils in the Bay Area that identifies with the smaller deeds, identify and reward people who exemplify the best of the best good-doers. You see, two different objectives. I happen to belong to the big enchilada and the smaller one -- the smaller one that fills my heart. Get it?"

"I get it. On the smaller fish, the non-advisory, to what council do you belong? Herb and Fausto are in the city, and you and Max are here in the East Bay. How's that?" inquired Walter. "Now, this is confusing to me."

"It is and it is not. Again, each of the eight councils are aligned in geographic areas. It is just for logic alignment and not service. Because we do not serve anyone. Max and I belong to Fausto's council for friendship. We get along so well. In fact, we are well regarded in the Bay Area federation of councils. That is all. And each council has cells, ranging from six to eight members. That is why our cell meets everywhere."

"Well explained. Therefore, your organization, the big gun, does a lot of good almost underground, with no fanfare, no publicity. I like it that way. And, it does not involve politics."

"I agree with your thinking. So, where were we? Were we talking about Sam?"

"Yes, you were talking about Max and then you veered to Sam," alerted Walter.

"Thinking of Sam..." Elvera forcing herself to recollect the intended details, just said ..." Oh, Sam is such a good man. What a human being God created."

"Has Sam ever revealed details of his past? I wonder why he chose the streets for his habitat! With too much riding on his reputation, he rejects any kind of overture to main street -- a place with a room and a bed. His buddy, what's his name?"

"You mean Randolph?"

"Yes, I just met him once. But he and Sam look like two peas in the same pod."

Elvera stopped. Walter had no questions to ask. Then, remembering what she intended to say in the first place, said:

"We learned some bits and pieces about his past from Sam. It is a combination of family past, back in Georgia and also a vocation thing -- doing good occupies all his time."

"Are you close enough to him to ask questions about dreams? Are you that close?"

"You mean ask Sam questions about dreams? Never crossed my mind. It would sound weird; I am not close to him as you imply. Actually, only Fausto is close to him. Sam slips through our grasp."

Walter just grinned and waited for more. "Nevertheless, why are we now investing so much talk on dreams? Dreams are like anything else in life. Everyone has them and encounters them. One has to feel comfortable sharing dreams as a way of getting a useful conversation started. Sam would be far-fetching. Not even Fausto, who deals with him almost every day, has a sure bridge to Sam."

"Okay, you have a plan."

Elvera just nodded, then stayed quiet, pensive. She conceded to herself that her dreams were compelling enough to merit a conversation marathon. Still, there was the possibility that they could fade away soon.

"Look, it is almost four o'clock. Do you want to go out for dinner? An early dinner?"

"Nah. I am still full from the brunch. How about going for a matinee to see a good movie on the big screen? And then decide on food. What do you say?"

"Okay! A movie again is not a bad idea."

"Let me google on what's available."

"That's a deal."

4

Fausto and Herbert

Adopting Sam

The best way to find yourself
Is to lose yourself in the service of others
----- Gandhi
Only a life lived for others is a life worthwhile
-----Einstein

Elvera called Fausto and listened to the typical recorded greeting stating he was away from his phone and that a message would be desirable. Text messaging would also be okay via his cell phone. Elvera quickly thought up an adequate reply that reflected her astute thinking, or thinking well on the fly: "This is your friend from the East Bay. Yes, with a woman's voice, perhaps the only woman in the East Bay that calls you for confession. Why bother with text messaging when e-mail would do the same? At least I could print your message if you lied to me. Sorry, Fausto, I am in a good mood. I just want to talk to you about a couple of issues. Greetings and peace!"

That was one of her important calls she had in mind right after she arrived from the long weekend away at her Monterey home. The dream, the enjoyable discussion of her dream with Walter and the need to proceed to other matters, gave her a bundle of energy and some sort of adrenaline towards finding additional answers to her concerns. Walter had cleared the shell covered pick-up truck and placed the coolers and plastic boxes in their right spots. They had to be parked in the right spots, for, after years of accumulating tools, plumbing and air conditioning parts in his garage, he gave them all up. Not really. He summoned two of his employees to clear the garage of unnecessary tools and parts out of there and reroute them to recycling places or transfer them to his business warehouse. He had succeeded in keeping it masterfully cleaned and organized to the point that sometimes friends, on short visits, would claim they would live in the garage year-round, or even have an occasional drinking party.

Arriving at two o'clock in the afternoon allowed Walter no time to either go to the shop or find a buddy for a nine-hole round of golf. He had not played golf at all for almost two weeks. The weather had been so-so and Elvera was on one of her spiritual journeys that now included a dream. He had hoped the conversation on the weekend would be the last chapter on his assignment as confidant and dream interpreter. Knowing Elvera's nature, he doubted that the end would be near. Actually, she had already begged him to recall some of his own dreams. *No way -- they are not pretty or perhaps they are scary.*

Elvera, while taking care of food for dinner, had called Father Fausto Mancini and then planned to call Pastor Herbert Hawkins. A certain plan was forming in her mind. Some upcoming assignments were on the calendar: a charity talk for a group of elderly women, and a presentation at a Catholic High School. The first would bring some dough for a Catholic Charity Foundation, and the latter would excite late teenagers -- high school seniors -- to give their all to worthy causes. Her mantra with these young people was that they should shy away from the usual clichés of *you are the future of society*, and, instead, render inspiration towards becoming *the now movers and shakers of the world*. She was adamant that they not only live their age but also be relevant: *look at me, I am almost on social security, taking more pills than milk, and losing my hearing. You are credible. Then, be relevant right now. Waiting for my age will not make the cut, for wisdom does not solve all the problems. Engagement and purpose will make a difference.*

She would continue and master her delivery with *Yeah, yeah, I am wiser now and can still do things others have not done yet. But you live in the now, not on older people's schedule. I also like to play bridge.* She would vary her speeches and interchanges and provide fresh ideas always. Nevertheless, she mostly defied and challenged the young folks to start acting and making a difference in the moment. *How long do you know you will live? Long! I hope. But no one knows.* The students always applauded her mini-speeches and challenged her to visit again with fresh ideas.

For Elvera, Fausto was the ideal parish priest without spending too much time in the building. He had a competent deacon who had retired from the banking industry, a parish secretary and a few volunteers that handled all the books and other needs. He also had a parish council that managed the simple church business; like a business. They possessed one uncanny attribute -- an ability to attract generous donors that would serve well two other parishes in Latin countries and in Africa. Father Fausto Mancini's was a small parish in the business district, with a typically lower number of parishioners. However, he had a generous number of visitors and Mass attendees during day-time. Besides visits to two hospitals, a funeral service every now and then, one assisted living and retirement center, member of a couple of semi-civic groups, Fausto's remaining time was around homeless environments. He always found time for the downtrodden or soup kitchen events. Elvera would label him a "missionary on wheels." He moved quickly from one environment to another almost effortlessly. She even remembered that one day a few months ago, she had partnered with Fausto, both dressed in clumsy clothing, in order to pay visits to their clients in the streets, like brother and sister or as a middle-aged husband and wife team. That was the one and only time she had come home totally vindicated. "This is living," she remembered saying it to Walter.

"Cheers, Vera. Relax. It was just a missed telephone call. You must have forgotten I have a cell phone; a good one and my only extravagance. You dialed the church's number instead. I suspect it is dinner time. You can call me after your dinner -- until midnight."

"Thanks Fausto. Walt had gone to the store and I was in the bathroom. Missed your call by a few seconds."

"Just like that. No secrets at all."

"What's there to hide?" He laughed, she did, too.

"How was the weekend in Monterey? Was the weather good? Did you play golf at Pebble Beach?"

"Pebble Beach? Me, on a retiree's budget?" Fausto laughed and she continued. "No. In my case, you know the best golf I play is being a good caddy. After eight misses I would pull the ball up and keep it in my pocket. You know, I avoid annoying Walt and his buddies because I take too many swings." Fausto understood and applauded her strategy. "Anyway, no time for golf; besides, some of Walt's buddies were away. But we had a good time, worthy of the area. We also took short and long walks, enjoyed the ocean breeze, a good movie and lots of chat with Walt." Elvera hesitated hitting Fausto with details about her dream. The importance of the dream could not be mixed with casual talk.

"I admire the way you and Walt are handling more free time together. Most people I come to know get very nervous and uncomfortable in having much time together, kind of invading each other's territory. It is a logical phenomenon -- invading space and time."

"You are correct. I know some couples that cannot take it without a fuss, or even some friction." Fausto sensed that Elvera had another justification for their getting along well. Indeed! "Remember that Walt finds time to visit the shop a few hours a day or when it pleases him. Golf and baseball games occupy his time as well. So, we naturally give some space to each other. And I am busy; and will always stay busy and involved. The rest of the time, which is plenty more, we spend discovering each other's secrets. We do have and cherish our independence as much as our togetherness."

"That is true. Lucky you and lucky everyone who benefits from your kindness and Walt's wits. Anyway, what's on the table?"

"We need to have a simple preparation for our potential meeting with professor Eichelberger. I am not saying all of us in the group, but at least you, Herb, and I need to meet for some preliminary conversation."

"Okay, I agree. And what do you have in mind? My schedule for this week is light and typical. In the next two weeks things get tight."

To Elvera, Fausto's light schedule meant there were no funerals to service, no meetings with Catholic Charities, or Sam was not in trouble. "Well, tomorrow I have an afternoon meeting in church and a speaking engagement at a Catholic High School on Friday. Wednesday and Thursday look good for me. I just need to call Herb. Unless..."

"... Unless I do it."

"Of course, you talk regularly. Being adversaries makes no difference to you."

Fausto just smiled; Elvera also could tell as he said: "Hold your accusation. Herb has his ideas and beliefs. Yet, we both deliver the goods and God so far has not told us to handle spiritual needs differently. I know you are joking." Elvera just sent a few sighs on her side of the line. "I take it you want us on your side of the Bay. That means we'll take BART and you pick us up at the Broadway station, just as we did a month ago."

"Right on. Thursday could be ideal; 11:30 in the morning I will pick up you gentlemen there." Silence followed until Elvera found courage to add the clincher, and no clincher. "Listen I will pay for lunch. Walt got a bonus from the company. The kids were very generous. Herb has money but your pockets are as clean as Sam's pockets."

"That's a deal. And taking alms comes with the territory. Herb rarely takes a pass either. I will call you if Herb cannot make Thursday. Okay?"

"Okay. See you Thursday."

∞∞∞∞∞

"You guys look spiffy, casual but modern. Did you board the same train?"

"No, but we talked over the phone. We were about eight minutes apart. I waited at the station," Herbert replied.

"So, you like my attire, matching Herb's. Fortunately, he carries no tie."

"Normally you do not tell jokes. It is my territory. Yet, I like a man (every now and then) who adds a tie to his repertoire of clothing. Now, you, Fausto are a surprise to me. The rags sporting 49ers ads needed to go. You don't look homeless, but fit for intellectual arguments." Both Herbert and Fausto could tell they were targeted for smart talk from and with Elvera.

"Shall we go back to the city, Herb? I sense we cannot match or are not ready for Vera's wit. She must have a plan. And we have had no advance notice. Talking about Eichelberger could have been accomplished by e-mail, anyway. Don't you agree, Herb?" Herbert just nodded and said:

"I do not talk your language. But enough of this BS. Where are we going? Fausto tells me Walt hit the jackpot. You are paying. Is that it?"

"No secrets, Fausto. Yes, I will be glad to splurge with you, eclectic folks. Let's walk to my car parked outside. I was lucky to have found a space on the street. And then let's drive to Emeryville. There is a good place to eat and talk; noisy but ideal for our chat."

"Eclectic?! Hanh! That's what we are now, brother Herbert -- eclectic." Herbert chuckled, Elvera offered a modest smile, but said in defense of the use of her adjective:

"Yes, you are. Both of you are. One is a Roman Catholic priest and the other a Lutheran minister. Both of you espouse different philosophies but are currently ecumenical partners, post Vatican II adherents."

"Ecumenical! Post Vatican II! Way past reformation. It took that long -- over four hundred years," noted Herbert.

"Let's go Vera, before you drown in your own adjectives. I can take a good (free) lunch," concluded Fausto.

∞∞∞∞∞

"Good place. Never been here. I did come before, a mile further, to Berkeley. The restaurant was famous for good Italian cuisine and sea food. I guess it is now closed or disappeared. Let me see... Spengers!" said Herbert.

"Never been in either," Fausto said.

"Fisherman's wharf was getting too expensive and too crowded," continued Herbert.

"I loved Spenger's sourdough bread. I would go there just for their bread and butter. One flaw, though: unless you enjoyed a good time at the bar, the wait at times was prohibitive. That is why these other two restaurants came to be; I guess. It is my take. Still, in typical honesty, I never had trouble finding a table. Walt knew at least two waiters that responded nicely to Walt's tips. I remember one saying -- 'your table is reserved, Mr. Betancourt. Follow me.' All the time. That is what I call 'who knows who.'"

They ordered the food. Fausto ordered a Ruben Sandwich with salad on the side and Herbert ordered a crab sandwich with French fries. Still undecided, Elvera ordered calamari steak with their delicious mashed potatoes and glazed string beans. All opted for chardonnay. Red wine, at lunch, would cause drowsiness. They wanted to talk about the meeting. Elvera did not care less for the professor's project; her dream was an exclusive matter camouflaged in project preparation.

"Cheers! To our friendship and now to Walt as well."

"Thanks, Vera. This is one of a few times I do not profess vows of poverty," said Fausto.

"In my case I am just honoring Jesus' miracle -- the changing of water into wine," confirmed Herbert. "And by the way, Fausto, did Jesus transform water into red wine or make the water taste like wine? Like this one, though white. Really good."

"You stumped me with such a question. I have no idea. In my seminary years, reading the Bible and learning more about the history of the times, I have no recollection about grape and wine choices. Yet, that area in the Mediterranean is not a haven for white wines. Anyway, we are not here to discuss viniculture."

"Your conversation or the subjects for conversation are always reasons for me to be excited about talking with you. You play your thoughts well and place bridges to heaven with such subtlety." She paused then added: "I was hungry."

Herbert also hinted he was enjoying his crab sandwich and then said: "I do not mind talking about professor Eichelberger's project. It has meaning. And by including us in the mix, it could improve the students' thesis in philosophy. Two religious professionals, one credible Catholic layperson and one capable Agnostic, must make a difference on their research. However, we need two more players to make up the number he suggested. Six students and six interviewees. Right?"

"Right," confirmed Elvera. "Max in, makes four and, two more outside the religious main stream, should provide a good balance." Elvera paused, thought further and added a provable clincher. "The professor had his thoughts on Sam. Having him as kind of a Mother Teresa without habits and religious connections, would guarantee great outcomes."

Fausto added: "Yes, it would be a home run. But he'll never show his face on matters like this one. No way! We need to find the missing pieces elsewhere. Sorry, Mr. Professor. A homeless person in the research would hit the papers like fireworks."

"Okay, I know Sam but not nearly as well as you two know him. He is kind of a hero to me -- that is all I know." She paused; Fausto and Herbert thought she had more on Sam. Instead she said: "I have an answer that can fill the voids."

"Go ahead; we trust you," said Herbert.

"It is almost a long shot, but it is worth a try. Walt could fit the mold of an unattached spiritual person, for he is a man with no religious attachments. He goes to Mass with me on Sundays and on special occasions. He has no religious trappings, can handle a conversation involving beliefs, etc. but, he is not like me. And, certainly like you. He will fit because, in spite of his superficial involvement in matters such as the ones we deal regularly, he respects his culture of the old country and sponsors anything that elevates the soul -- human beings. In other words, his Christian traditions are ingrained in him; his achievements have been balanced with pride and modesty. Which means he can deliver common sense."

She paused as the two waited for their moment. "He has just a high school education and a few courses at a junior college. Nonetheless, he reads his stuff. I like what he reads. And he, initially pushing my idea away, will cave in. I know that."

"Did you finish? You can go on; but I am sold on the idea. Relevancy wins me all the time. Bring him in."

"Thanks Herb. I suspect you will agree, Fausto."

"Of course, I do. He is recruited. We still need one more."

"I will fix it, too. We need another woman. There'll be female students in the game. Perhaps a ratio of forty-sixty percent. Do you think so?"

"Nowadays, yes. You Catholics still remain stuck on no-women priests. However, women are equally engaged on philosophy." Fausto dismissed Herbert's bait.

∞∞∞∞∞

They were savoring the last pieces of their food. Elvera had a thought about two not yet fully identified players in the group of six. She opened the talk:

"I am still thinking about the players. We are in as well as Max. The other two depend on my convincing them to also join. My friend would fit quite well and Walt could enlist and provoke some laughs -- Archie Bunker style. Can you add anything to this; in case I do not succeed?"

"I should not worry about this thing. The professor will be happy with us four. I guess Fausto will not worry about it, either. Right?" retorted Herbert.

Father Mancini's silence was indicative of, so far, Elvera could deliver the correct players to add relevancy to the professor's project. Elvera added: "This is it, then."

"Really? How can you be so sure that Fausto has said his peace? Besides our thought in including Sam?"

Elvera replied: "His silence tells me he defers his choices to us. He's a busy man and I suspect he could find someone that would adequately fit in with us. He would name Sam if it fit the bill. Isn't that it, Herb?" Fausto Mancini was still enjoying what was left of his sandwich, while exchanging smiles with Herbert and Elvera.

"Okay Herb. It sounds like you know him quite well, too; you know his environment and secrets. However, you two have been friends for some time, I guess. I have known you folks for just two years. Did you know each other before you knew me?"

Mancini said: "You are talking about him, not Sam?!" Elvera nodded yes. "Herb, up close … not more than two years. Maybe three. I had seen him in our organization for some years; but never close. Remember BaDR (Be a Difference Rainbow) is not small. We cover the whole Bay Area."

"I know. How did this happen that you became like twins?" asked Elvera.

"Tell her, Herb." Herbert agreed.

"Strange ways, or God's ways. It was through my brother-in-law, a Chicago resident. It will take long to at least do it justice. It involves Sam, too."

"I have time and this sounds like a rich find. How about you, Fausto?" said Elvera.

"Go ahead Herb. Start the story. My phone has not rung yet; no messages. Like Elvera suggested, we can get coffee. Vera pays the bill and we move to the bar."

Elvera for sure was experiencing excitement beyond her expectations. After all, these missionaries of the street were also funny.

∞∞∞∞∞

Edmund Conrad walked side by side with what he thought was a homeless person. His clothes were shabby, not smelly, dirty or even tattered. He had met him with another homeless person -- perhaps buddies -- on the street. Both were not sitting as most homeless did -- their backs against the wall, slumped on their knees, eyes semi-closed, holding a wrinkled brown paper bag housing a bottle of Bronco wine. Their eyes were semi-open as they extended their hands for small change or begging for food. Food or money for food was the customary cover for something else. Maybe if they changed the routine -- like a new marketing idea -- they would have more success. It would be worth a try. But his, now walking together companion, had to be homeless. After all, he was in San Francisco, close to downtown or thereabouts, in one of those many streets crossing Mission and/or Market streets. As beautiful and quaint San Francisco was, homelessness was an additional fixture -- many times an overblown fixture. He knew that because his brother-in-law had indicated in so many words what San Francisco had accomplished in combating the ever-growing population of homeless folks.

He still did not know why he spontaneously followed this homeless person; he did not know his name and or felt motivated to ask or entertain introductions. Then, when they met, he was oblivious to any method of introductions between a homeless person and him -- this upstanding and relatively well-off Chicagoan and visitor to the City by the Bay. After meandering through almost a dozen blocks -- still not aware of any valid reason -- and almost silently following this homeless person without a name, he came to a halt at a church. Yes, a Catholic Church. I guess, directly in the middle right side of the street.

The church, if it had displayed no name, could be taken for any other building. Of course, the church bell-tower provided some sort of a distinct feature, a different use. It could also be that the homeless was a disguised, an undercover Catholic priest, now ready to convert him to his flock. A Lutheran himself, mildly involved in his own church, he could be an easy prey. Certainly, he had to be easy catch for he still was unsure of this act of agreeing to follow this San Franciscan homeless which he soon would come to know as the priest or one of the priestly cohorts. The church's sign was visible, the façade looked okay. It was clean, absent of any decrepit material or begging for repairs or revealing an old and cold past. Just like the rest of the buildings surrounding this church. The door of the smaller -- one floor only -- building adjacent to the church opened up after the homeless' two soft knocks. A male, perhaps in his late forties or fifties, with curly black hair, now somewhat unruly from the day's activities, dressed in a faded black and gold distinctively 49er sweatshirt and grey, also worn sweatpants, opened the door, greeted the homeless guy with a broad smile and uttered the most likely usual greeting:

"Good afternoon, Sam." Sam stayed motionless like absentminded or lost for greetings, a reciprocation of sorts. "Yes, good afternoon. It's already four o'clock; very strange to see you this late on a Monday, following the last Sunday of the month .... what's happening, partner?"

I guess I was right -- a partner in the begging business, thought Edmund.

Edmund was not hurt that he was being ignored -- unceremoniously ignored. Both the man in the 49er-attire and the homeless man (still for now homeless man) had not acknowledged his presence in any typical or perhaps awkward fashion. Edmund waited and waited more. Well, he recognized that the homeless man had not yet answered the "what's happening" question from the 49er-dressed-and-undercover-for-sure priest.

Then, while certain there would be no answer and receiving an equally broad and warm smile, Edmund got the answer he had waited for. "Are you two together?" Both -- the homeless and Edmund -- nodded yes.

Addressing Sam and not losing sight of Edmund, the supposed priest added: "What is the catch this time? A Montgomery Street Executive businessman? A wealthy donor?" Edmund chuckled, while the homeless just smiled meekly. "C'mon, what's the deal, Sam?"

Now Edmund knew the disguised homeless had a name — "Sam." How nice, a comfortable and cozy name. Sam replied: "No, he isn't San Franciscan. He's a tourist -- a very generous tourist." Sam paused and then followed with the clincher reply: "You know, I need your help. He wants to give me one-hundred dollars."

"One-hundred dollars? Hah, that's nice. Don't you know his name?" Sam shook his head -- indicating a perfect no. "Didn't you ask? The right mannered gent forgot to follow his own rule?"

The disguised priest's speech was supported by an Italian-type hand gesticulation, a traditional on-going ribbing, a lovely scolding. All in the same motion. Sam looked down somewhat meekly and somewhat mischievously. At least his contrite smile looked mischievous. Now directing his total attention to Edmund, the presumed priest offered his hand and said: "I'm Fausto Mancini -- the pastor of this church. And you sir? Gracing this encounter with your presence and taken for a ride by this man, Mr. Sam Williams."

Edmund appeared lost, Father Mancini rescued him: "And your name?" *Is this priest joking, is he a jester, or has he taken an afternoon shot of tequila?* thought Edmund. *Maybe he does comedy on the side.*

Okay, Edmund had the first guess revealed. The man with curly, disheveled hair was a priest without a habit. And he was jovial, plain old vanilla. Perhaps he was a successful apostle of the church. "My name is Edmund Conrad. I don't know why I am here with...." pointing to Sam he continued ... "now I know he is Sam. Yes, with Sam. I just followed him." Edmund hesitated, then said: "he said I had to meet you before I handed him a few bucks, my donation. I had no idea it would be to a church."

"Sorry for asking, are you uncomfortable with that? Money for the church?"

Edmund ventured no answer. He was the donor and required no justification for an offer from his hard-earned money. Usually nothing would floor him or cause any sort of stuttering. However, what had developed so far was news to him, and it came faster than he expected. "I don't know what to say." He paused and then decided to take charge: "Gosh it's no big deal, not a lot of money, anyway. What's the point? I just met you and I don't know anything about Sam. As far as I could tell he's..."

"A homeless? Anyone can say that. Of course, he is. But one with a significant and lovely difference. Thank God for that." Edmund was relieved the homeless had some credentials in the begging business. Father Mancini continued. "Let me share some details. Sam is what he is, a great human being." *He changed tones with such ease - from comedian and now to a preacher. Of course, he must preach his sermons.* Edmund's brain was racing with configurations of this priest's mode of conversation. The chat was definitely out of his league. "All the big money he comes to collect is dropped with me. He does have a place but not with the safe arrangements to keep money. The money is his for whatever the good things he does. I am like his bank. He drops money and gets money when he needs and asks. Meantime, we're friends and I love hearing his stories of mercy, which never exceed a dozen words."

"Thank you, thanks for sharing; now I know. Is Sam connected with your church?"

"No, he is not. He's his own boss and master. If you get what I mean, he's a servant of God even if he does not acknowledge it or tell it."

Edmund Conrad was not confused. Just surprised at becoming a witness to a warm if not a slowly developing intriguing story, by an intriguing and funny priest. Father Mancini was reading Edmund's conflict well and offered a more definitive thought: "No, Sam is not a 'homeless' by fate alone. Or by design, if there is some vocation or divine intervention in the mix." *Big words, philosophical statements I'm not used to; well, unless I'm in the company of Herbert*, thought Edmund.

Then, looking sideways at Sam and just to make sure his next question was appropriate, Edmund said. "Okay, that is a good summary of Sam's good character. Tell me more. I may like to hear more descriptions or stories about Sam." In truth, Edmund had plenty of time. He was just enjoying this freelance tourist stroll through the city now with funny twists. Sam, however, appeared uncomfortable with the usual praise coming from Father Mancini and now piggy-backed by Mr. Conrad. He kind of slowly danced around as his feet tip-toed and slowly swirled. Both Father Mancini and Edmund Conrad took note of that, almost laughing. It had to mean many things, including Sam's apparent reluctance to hear additional praise.

Father Mancini put a softer spin in his story. "Well, Sam has a place to stay. He just chooses to be around those he knows he can help and get results."

Edmund's curiosity increased. He thought he would learn something that is rarely shared in normal conversations or everyday news and in an apparent safe environment -- near or at the door of a church, a house of God. Nothing that could go viral in social media was equally worth knowing. Yet, he was being introduced to Father Mancini only for a specific purpose -- Sam's purpose. Not as an invited guest for a chat or for a fact-finding story.

"I sense that Sam is ready to go, ready to continue his work. I have a little time. Do you care for some tea?"

Sam was ready to leave but waited to see if Mr. Conrad accepted the tea invitation or chose to walk back with him to the spot of their initial encounter. Seeing no immediate action, he looked at Father Mancini and hinted he had a question.

"I know, you're late and think I forgot you. I did not." Sam's smile was no longer meek. It was as broad as his eyes now revealed. "I have three bags for you. They contain good stuff; of course, with irrelevant expired dates. At least two bags of Lays potato chips are in the bags. Do you want to take some now or tomorrow? It does not matter that it is one more day old."

"Not now. I've got to catch up with other business. Randolph and me will come tomorrow morning. Thank you. Always thank you."

"Sure... I thank you, too." Sam, guessing Mr. Conrad would stay for tea, waved goodbye to Father Mancini and extended his two hands to Mr. Conrad's own hand, warmed it with a pious smile and vanished. Sam's hands looked as clean as his posture.

Sam was already on his way out when Father Mancini yelled at him: "If you show up after the seven-thirty Mass I will have warm pancakes and hot chocolate for both of you. Unless someone needs spiritual help. You know what I'm talking about." Sam knew it well. Sometimes Father Mancini would thank him for coming at the right moment -- interrupting him from tiring schmoozing -- the daily dose from old parishioners.

Now alone and still on the side walk, Edmund Conrad hoped Father Mancini would renew the offer for a cup of tea. *Not yet? he thought.* "You see, more than a year ago Sam was offered shelter at a large home subsidized by a Lutheran Church here in the city." Mr. Conrad's gaze almost froze -- *a Lutheran Pastor,* he murmured? "The Pastor had met Sam and also me at a charitable gathering. He became spellbound by Sam's heroics for being awarded the be-a-difference-man of the year recognition. It was a humbling thing at this low key and overly secular organization."

Father Mancini could not read the effect of his words on Edmund. Conrad's face had changed colors and expression. That caused Father Mancini to rush a concluding remark. "The Lutheran Pastor offered him a permanent shelter; modest as many shelters are, but a good shelter."

"Forgive me for interrupting," said Edmund Conrad while smiling and hoping Sam had not gone out so fast and away from his sight. No luck. "Can you tell me the name of the Lutheran Pastor?"

Then added: "Could he be someone by the name of Herbert Hawkins?"

"Yes," said Father Mancini with a surprised, mostly dumbfound look. "How do you know this? You just met Sam a few moments ago? Isn't it true?"

"I guess I can accept a cup of tea now. Is it still an offer?" Father Mancini smiled and allowed him to proceed.

"Of course! And are you sure you can have a long chat?"

Father Mancini's progressive smile was a little disconcerting for Edmund, so he concluded: "Why not? This must be part of your ministry. Yes?"

"Sure, come in."

As both walked from the door onto the narrow hallway Father Mancini explained: "Sam is truly unique. He's the best example of natural humility. I value this so much because it is the most difficult virtue for me to handle." Then, taking a breather, added: "Pastor Hawkins was also touched by Sam's transparent and virtuous behavior." He paused again. "So, even far away, you know Herb Hawkins?"

"Of course, I do. You don't know this but he married my daughter last Saturday."

Father Mancini stopped, looked straight into Edmund's eyes and said: "Really? What a small world! Of course, we're far away and yet close. Miraculous," retorted Father Mancini.

He chose the moment to explain the meaning of the three rooms surrounding the hallway. There was a little office with bookcases, a desk, two chairs and other memorabilia. Another small room had a couch, a single kneeling prayer pew, another modest size bookcase. The walls were covered with pictures of some icons, including ones of two popes, and the prominent wooden cross hanging from the wall. The third room was a makeshift dining area with a dining table for four, five chairs. The dining room had a large opening in the wall that lead to a small kitchen. It had again a small counter with a sink and a faucet, two small cabinets with dishes, glasses, and a useful refrigerator. Other minor kitchen utensils completed the entertainment arrangement. Beyond these, there were two small bedrooms with a shared full bathroom.

Father Mancini excused himself and walked towards the kitchen where water was boiling. Conrad could tell, for the hissing from the kettle was intensifying in noise. Tea was served, sipped as they warmed themselves to some juicy revelations -- all about Sam.

"Sam rarely uses the shelter except for a nap. I guess during the day, as most occupants are out, he goes there to his room, takes care of things he needs to take care, including interacting with the impromptu shelter users. He even cooks occasionally. Like the food I set aside, food with labels showing an expiration date." Edmund Conrad was in authentic if not virtual listening mode, and signaled Mancini to go on. "You see, cans of ravioli, beans, uncooked pasta and other items. He shares the food with some people at the shelter and the others, his friends on the streets, under the freeways, in alleys and unused spots."

"I meant to ask you about the bags of food -- expired food value. Do you also feed the homeless?"

"Oh, those bags!? We, at the church -- I guess most churches perpetually ask their flock to bring food -- ask and receive non-perishable stuff and other items every last Sunday of the month. Yesterday was that Sunday. Most food is sent away to food pantries, shelters for battered women. You name it. However, we're careful in not sending away food that show severely expired dates. Church volunteers sort it all on Monday."

"That's a shame for some food is still good, still edible" Edmund interjected.

"You're right. And I know of tons of food that are thrown away. Those dates are phony."

"How come?"

"Easy. Most dates reflect the merchandise turn over in stores. Not the shelf value. Besides some of these shelters receive government subsidies. Allowing expired date food does not sit well with the government. It's a catch twenty-two thing."

"So, some of the expired food is given to Sam?"

"Correct. Sam always comes early Monday. He was late this time and thought I would forget him."

"Does Sam attend church services? You call these services attending Mass?"

"No, he does not. I do not know if he's religious or what religion, if any, he belongs to. One thing I have noticed or caught him a few times doing is waiting for me when I return late from other errands. I catch him in the church, in those back pews, just thinking or meditating. He feels awkward when I catch him still, like enjoying a quiet moment."

"So, you never talked with him about religion."

"Never. It wouldn't matter. We both understand the language of silence and mutual respect. Deeds speak for ourselves."

Edmund Conrad was feeling that special spiritual lift. His eyes were fixated on every word Father Mancini uttered; like the eyes could listen or talk. Mancini continued: "I wish I could be as useful and relevant as he is."

"You like him?"

"Certainly, I do. It is easy to love and admire that human being."

"How did you come to know him? The same way as Herbert? At this gathering?"

"Oh, no. A long time ago. Let me see, seven or ten years ago. Maybe longer than that."

"It makes sense -- long ago. The way you two talk with or to each other, it conveys a long and solid friendship. Was he homeless then? No family?"

"Okay, that is a long sentence."

Edmund smirked a genuine smile; his lips revealed the difference between a smile and smirking.

"Let me get the order of things here. First with me: I was ordained at age thirty-two; in Boston. I'm a Dominican priest, you see." Edmund could not tell the difference between a Dominican priest or any other." Right before my hitting twenty-eight, knowing and living the ABCs of life and totally unsure what to do next, I decided to become a priest, to do things for others. Then fresh from being ordained I was assigned to teach at a Catholic High School -- teach and become the school chaplain."

Edmund intervened: "Do you do any teaching now? Pastors must be so busy and do not have enough time to teach?"

"No, I do not teach. In fact, after a few years I didn't feel fit to do that. The assignment was too easy and the students were smart, motivated, from balanced and upper middle-class families. I needed some challenge, I needed tough environments. You know, I was an idealist. One of the vows we are asked to take is humility. Idealists are rarely humble. Then, at my request, I transferred to a New York parish and a grammar school. I saw the light there because the area was an inner-city environment with poor working-class families."

Edmund interrupted father Mancini. "You are here now. Being an idealist, you found an environment to live your dream or your calling. What got you to come here? Pardon me for being nosy."

"No, I don't mind talking about me. I already know much about you. And, oh, and your cousin Herbert. Here is the rest of my story about being here. A few years later -- around my early forties -- another priest I had known before, recommended I come to San Francisco -- to a parish that needed someone with an Italian name and fit to work with a mix of rich and some people not so rich, border line poor. The community was changing."

"So, you speak Italian?" asked Edmund.

"Are you kidding? Because I said 'Italian name'? That was a joke: I just talk with my hands and a word or two. I'm happy, though. Stay with me, I'm close to getting to Sam. During those years, I was still idealistic, but not fond of rigid schedules. Being an assistant Pastor with some free time, fit my choices. I would venture to the areas where many homeless congregated. I felt I belonged there -- at least in my free time. That is where I met Sam. He was as dysfunctional as one can get. There is no need for glamorous details. I learned he had been in Vietnam, got wounded with shrapnel on his left side." He paused to give an example: "Did you notice the left side of his face? Some parts do not have beard. His body's left side has scars all over. So, even wounded but recuperated, he decided to rejoin until the war ended in the mid-seventies. He took odd jobs here and there but never settled in anything. His wife and child deserted him and his life went south. I mean ... they got tired of him. He came to San Francisco, joined some of his buddies, perhaps veterans from the service. Bad company. Vietnam ruined many good people. The carnage to which they were witness was also too much for their young minds. He disintegrated and homelessness became his life."

"Sad story. The nation will never know the true impact of vicious wars. Vietnam was one of them. Iraq is another one. We will never know." Edmund paused. Father Mancini appeared finished. Edmund still was a question or two away. "So, you met him in the dumps. How about his family? Did they reconnect? Does he receive government benefits?"

"As far as I came to know, he never tried to reconnect with his family. He never allowed me to address that subject. I respected his privacy. Yes, he receives Veteran benefits, but not as much as he should or is entitled to. He messed it up when he rejoined the second time. After all he had been wounded. In any case the meager benefits are gone by the third week. All to help his clients. If he had more, he would give more and to more people."

"The way I see, you are a hero. You helped him find himself and a way to be useful."

"With the exception of the hero thing, you're right on all the things you said. A miracle my friend?! No. He does his thing better than anyone else. He is like family without the usual visits or connections. In other words, I can say we are very close with few words."

The stories appeared too raw, too true but equally a blessing to Edmund Conrad. Father Mancini went on: "Back to the shelter -- the one Sam uses. The house accommodates close to eighteen people; or more on Winter days. The house is divided into four bedrooms, with two bathrooms for all. Each large bedroom, with bunk beds, sleeps six and the other is tiny. That's Sam's quarters. Even if he rarely sleeps there."

"And why does Sam do that and sleep on the streets?"

"I call Sam the Mother Teresa of the homeless. He's smart. But he is a true missionary without an official mission or a missionary organization. It is during the night that he does his work: talks, asks, tells, instructs and above all, kind of influences behavior changes in those he knows can do it."

Father Mancini stopped to reconfigure his own question. "You mentioned you met him with another homeless. Right?" Edmund Conrad nodded yes. "That other homeless had to be Randolph, a former homeless man who was down on his luck and doing drugs. Now he's like an assistant to Sam. That is what I call them: Master and apostle." Both laughed. "Their mission -- well, I coined it a mission -- is to rehabilitate everyone that they come across. And they do this with true modesty. Only a few cops know the story. He threatens them to stay silent -- a small price for his heroics to stay on. Otherwise, he would run away. He's done that once before. The cops know better."

"So, Herbert learned about Sam and did his good deed towards Sam. Sam, by all measures, is someone that the world should know about," blurted Edmund Conrad.

"It has to be on Sam's terms. Sam is astute and knows the world so well. He hates politics, and he disdains charity for show or for tax write-offs. He's principled to the core."

Edmund Conrad rubbed his hands, reached for the rest of the tea and waved his head right and left two times. Father Mancini smiled, too. Then added: "it's getting late for you. Yet I'm curious. Herbert married your daughter at his church?"

"Oh, no. I live in Chicago. Actually, in a suburb of Chicago. He's married to my sister. My daughter is attending Berkeley to get her degree in law, she found the love of her life and decided to get married."

"I see, nothing unusual. America is so mobile. Are you returning to Chicago soon?"

"Not yet; next week. The whole family entourage from our area is going to Yosemite tomorrow. After that, we will travel along the coast to Santa Monica. And then return to San Francisco for just a day and a night before going back to Chicago. Just enough time to confront Herbert on extending a hand to Sam."

"That's good. I sense Pastor Hawkins has changed a bit since I first met him up close at that gathering. He appeared then as a self-absorbed religious person. He was well mannered, well dressed, like an executive. Now he's more engaged and detached from the formalities. Even his attire has changed."

"I know what you mean. I noticed that change, too. He's looser, far more gregarious, less guarded, less cautious. With the wedding thing and many guests -- out of town guests -- it was difficult to chat with him more intimately. I like his demeanor now. I will learn more next week."

"Where was the wedding ceremony? At Hawkins' church?"

"No, it was not. My daughter's fiancée, I mean that's her husband now, is of Italian descent and naturally Catholic. It was at his Catholic Church near the Golden Gate Park. It was a dual officiating thing. Very well done."

"I see, another miracle in ecumenical partnership. God must be smiling.... Me, too."

"I guess you're right. The world needs more unity and fewer divisions," replied Edmund.

Both appeared having had their fill of meaningful conversation. Anything beyond now would be superfluous chat. It was getting close to six pm, too. Edmund Conrad was surprised he had received no calls from his wife who after lunch decided to go shopping with the other two couples. Edmund thought that breaking away from the group, preferring to do free-lance walking through downtown, gave him the better part. Thus, he experienced no regrets. Still he worried the phone had not rung. He excused himself for a moment, pulled the tiny *I-phone* from his shirt pocket, looked at it and noticed multiple messages: voice and text. He swung his head twice in disbelief. Then said: "Well you may have other souls to convert and I have to answer to my wife and our friends."

Getting the message, Father Mancini stood up. Edmund just murmured the word *souls*. He seldom used this or similar words in typical conversations. However, this was not a typical conversation.

"Well, I'm elated for having been exposed to small but real miracles. Of course, Sam -- like the miracle with you -- anything can be expected."

"It is not a big deal. I enjoyed talking with you."

Edmund Conrad nodded in some sort of agreement with the priest's thinking, then asked: "Can we exchange e-mail addresses? Do you e-mail?" He got a yes nod. "I also did enjoy your company and hospitality. And above all, now our being touched by Sam."

"Indeed, Sam has that talent and God given vocation. It was a blessing meeting you and I shall have a word with Hawkins once we meet again in two weeks."

"Do that. My wife and I are set to have dinner with him next week before we depart to Chicago. I'll grill him. Starting with a lie --- all about the homeless in San Francisco."

"Yes, homeless in the City by the Bay."

Before leaving Father Mancini's place, Edmund opened his wallet and extracted two fifty-dollar bills. "Look here. Please put this in Sam's treasury. Don't tell him a thing. You can do that, can't you?"

"Of course. On the other hand, I have a better idea. I will go out with Sam, check his work and buy a couple hamburgers for us, with French fries and coke."

"You're funny. Unlike Hawkins."

"By the way, before I let you go, where and how did you find Sam? Was he begging?"

"Not really. It was around one of these streets crossing Market and Mission. Like now, the afternoon was warm. There were lots of beggars; some did not look good at all."

"Never mind, you and I broke the ice. Tell the truth ... they looked dirty and may have annoyed people. I can take any comments, Conrad."

"Oh, I am not bashful in stating what I feel and what I saw. Many as you stated: disjointed, disconnected from the world. However, Sam was not. Actually, I found him with another fellow, both standing near the corner of those streets. They looked at me, smiling as a matter of fact. As you know, they did not dress like clean folks strolling on the street. Their smile caused me to be brave and ask a question. I was looking for a cigar shop that had been referred to me. They promptly told me where it was. In fact, they said: 'we are going in that direction. Follow us.' And I did; and I found the store. I thanked them and had the courage to ask them if they were homeless. Mind you, I did not ask them if they lived or worked nearby; but if they were homeless..."

"That is ironic. Well, you are a good, honest person, too."

"Thanks. They said they were homeless. At that moment I felt bad and meant to amend my error by fetching for my wallet. They just waited as my twenty-dollar bill caught their joy. Sam said 'please, buy your cigars and then follow us to a MacDonald's, buy us some hamburgers for our brothers that can't move well.' I did buy my stuff and then followed them to a MacDonald's. With twenty-five dollars I bought them over a dozen cheese burgers and bags of fries. The other fellow took the bags and left. I stayed temporarily with Sam until it was time for me to go. Sam, with his eyes almost wet, thanked me and said: 'you're a good man.'"

"Oh, yes, he can't hide his charm all the time. Good story. Then you handed him the one hundred-dollar bill. Is that it?"

"You got it. As I showed him the bill, he hesitated with the palms of his hands up. Instead he asked me to follow him. I did and did not ask questions. I just let the events take me over. I have no regrets -- none whatsoever."

"Now you have another friend. Thanks for sharing the story. *Arrivederci*," finished Father Mancini. Edmund Conrad just saluted the affable and funny priest.

∞∞∞∞∞

The story by Herbert Hawkins had concluded; Elvera was full of unusual emotions. "My Lord, my dear Lord. No wonder you are two peas in a pod. That was so wonderful."

"Indeed, we respect and admire each other. We are blessed with Sam, too," said Hawkins.

"No wonder that you both kind of adopted Sam."

"That is a good way to put the matter to a warm rest."

"Well, it is time to go. Walt must be worried, too."

"Are you cooking tonight?" asked Fausto Mancini.

"No way. I am full and we have good left-overs. Walt will not mind."

5

Max and his
Uncle Frederick

I loved my uncle Frederick
My father was very proud of him

Religion is the opium of the people
------ Karl Marx
If there were no God, there would be no atheists
------ G. K Chesterton

I graduated from high school without the benefit of graduation ceremonies. It was not a big deal, for college graduation, four years later, became a good replacement for the absence of companionship and face-to-face teachers at a typical high school. Or, so I thought. As surrogate teachers -- those class seniors and smart cookies -- did the job instead. It did not bother me, for I had been trained to learn for and by myself.

The friends I had while I walked the (home) virtual high school steps were few and our neighborhood in SF did not have many other families with kids like us -- my younger sister and me. Therefore, we had no one else to compare. It did not matter for I trusted my mom and respected my father; certainly, I had to fear my grandfather. His love was always connected with extolling the virtues of thinking and doing things by and for ourselves and dismissing the overly regimented crowd. My grandpa also promised that in time we would find others who would espouse the same belief.

Yes, my mom taught me since grade four. She had the time; and, in part, she had been pressured by my grandfather to provide an education free of any environment of religion -- whether superficial or obvious. Even public schools could be marginally trusted. My sister, though, went to a private school, somewhat favorable to my grandpa's taste and subsidized, in full, by him. My mother's income now relegated to tutoring English literature -- British and American -- was not enough for private school. Of course, I was a good student, well taught and obedient -- willing to follow instructions. My dad helped. If he were a little disappointed for me not benefitting from the high school environment, he made up with being my pal many times. My mom was also great with many trips to the library, museums and occasional attendance at local plays. These, however, were a small part of an arsenal of tools allowing me to achieve academic excellence. I also remember my father taking me to two basketball games around play-off time. My mother afterwards said that these would also add value to other aspects of learning. Who could forget basketball finals -- SF Warriors against the Chicago Bulls -- before Michael Jordan era? Yes, at the Cow Palace!!! What a thrill! Moreover, when the academic learning became center stage, nothing could beat my mom's skills and patience. I was well prepared to face and master college education.

My father, far from being meek, was compliant, obedient to my grandfather's dictates. He rarely would make waves. Yet, unlike my grandfather, he was far from being an atheist. Despite my grandfather's perennial influence, he married later than many young lads of his time. His wife, by being docile, calm and neutral in many causes and beliefs, became a ticket for some peace for my dad. Indeed, in an apparent attempt to start an emancipation of sorts, he promptly became a father of two in less than four years. I was the first. And then, two years later, my sister added to the joy of a family of a boy and a girl. That was enough for my parents to give up on the idea of a much larger family. Then there was a very curious and fascinating element in the equation. My uncle Frederick! Younger than my father by two years and some change, my uncle inherited my grandpa's DNA only in terms of drive, vitality, go-go motion and energy. As far as beliefs or no-beliefs, it stopped there. Obedient while under the control of my grandfather, uncle Frederick (rarely heard Fred as his name) gave up any doctrine my grandfather tried to instill in him. Actually, that doctrine was just listened to and discarded promptly. He had that ability of not making waves or, if confronted with waves, possessed a cunning ability to toss them out at the first chance he could find, including leaving no traces in the trash can. My father could, but did not. In addition, that behavior and occasional conversations with my dad were enough to cause my father's neutrality. It also became my own doctrine -- neutrality. However, I was my grandpa's favorite and docile grandson just as my father was all his life -- fearing to upset him. I was his project, and the clay he tried to mold into a follower. Yet, trying as he did, the end result, at best, landed me on a world of perennial ambiguity. Dogmas and ideals were generally difficult to reconcile with the world's unrelenting reality. Thus, I learned how to accept double standards and values well. I confess that I am still a work in progress.

My uncle Frederick was as nice as he was fearless and was the owner of a great heart. He was a good athlete, but without any scholarships because he loved many sports -- baseball, basketball and football in all of which he was good, but never attained excellence in any. At a little over six feet tall, he could be a bull; but was not. I loved him. I regret I saw very little of him. Even with four cousins, my dealings with them were rare, very scattered. Only after my grandfather's death did I get to know them and more about them. By then, with many of them spread around the state and the country, it was very difficult to maintain close relationships. I never told them to their faces or whispered in their ears that I loved them all. I suspect they understood that via some other channels. They were plain vanilla with shades of chocolate and strawberry; but were outstanding human beings, just like my uncle and his wife Josefina. Undeniably, she was a warm and gracious lady of Italian background, with a healthy gusto of *abundanza*. Even if my grandfather could recognize my uncle and aunt Josefina's easy-going lifestyle, he rarely would comment on it or much less give his blessings. Their life was as typical as anyone else's, with small successes and trivial mistakes, with ups and downs. But above all, they understood that happiness was an inside job – what you made with what you had and not what you possessed.

Had we lived closer I would perhaps have veered towards the road that my uncle turned. Marrying in the Catholic Church just to please my Aunt Josefina was the only thing close to going to church or espousing any other belief. It was not that important to him or that he could be influenced by my aunt's regular goings to church services -- like Sunday Mass. But as success in my uncle's business grew, my uncle wanted to have a family that lived like a family, like going to church even if little or nothing were expected from the event. School

-- a good and with sound practices school -- was very important to him; so were sports and other activities that would place kids together. His business sponsored little league teams and, when soccer became the thing with kids, he also got involved in fund raising events. If he had lived in the Midwest, in a small-town, he would be the unofficial mayor. He would be the cheerleader and sponsor-in-chief. In Santa Rosa, it did fit well also. Though public schools were good, influence from the other parents and even his business partner, my uncle took a chance on Catholic School for my cousins. Slowly, one by one, my three male cousins went to Catholic middle and high schools. My youngest female cousin by then started in kindergarten. It was the worst affront done to my grandfather. Ironically the confrontation erupted at a Thanksgiving dinner. Afterwards, my father labeled that confrontation between my uncle and grandfather, after the dinner, to be an "Ok Corral" fight. At that time, my grandmother had just passed away and her typical *let's-go-home-dear-stop-the-arguments* thing was no longer available for dismissing the fight or bringing it to a complete stop. My grandfather was empty of any of his own weapons and my grandmother's support. My father helped, but a little too late. My uncle rejoiced in the fight but never rubbed any noses thereafter. He had the ability to forgive and forget. He was a lifer.

"How's your health dad? Still very active with your writings and preaching?"

"What is on your mind?" He would never talk our language like "what do you mean, what's cooking." Even as a friend of workers, the ones with fewer rights, the ones marginalized by the wealthy barons, he rarely used language other than close to academia.

"Well, since mom passed away you need to slow down, smell the roses, and visit more with your grandchildren." I was close to sixteen and my dad was near fifty, and my grandpa past seventy. So, my uncle's advice was logical. Not to my grandfather. He was not finished -- not yet or ever.

"Not the way you are raising your kids. You're succumbing to the drug of religion. I raised you well, free of drugs and booze." That *salvo* had no reason to be fired. Even worse than the first shot in Lexington, done only accidentally. The Americans were ready to emancipate themselves, but in a calm and negotiable manner and were not rushed to war with the British by an accidental firing of a rifle. That mistake turned out well even if at the loss of many lives and perturbing grudges. My grandpa's salvo was not an accident. He wished for that moment a long time before. He was like the British who were in charge at will; no room for regrouping. Perhaps my uncle was equally ready. Yet, I never knew him for holding grudges, start fights or lighting matches. Not him. He would fight for survival the same way he fought in the last stages of the Vietnam War; he had been a decorated war hero -- for valor under fire; and he saved some of his buddies by putting his own life on the line. Therefore, he was ready for another fight, albeit word for word, gesture for gesture, with his opponent, his own father. This time -- too bad.

"Dad, why this kind of talk? I also did go to high school and graduated from college and learned social sciences, history and you name it. I know who said that religion is the opium of society. He did fight for the underprivileged working class and what not. His statement had some meaning. But he was a nobody. A marginal philosopher that earned many sympathizers and fomented many revolutions. But that is all. There isn't much the world has learned from which it has prospered. None of his doctrines are making news now."

"You are stating historical outcomes and some facts that one cannot sweep away. Many alive today cannot remember them that much, or have added their name to the history," replied my grandfather. He may have said something with better and more eloquent words than mine now. But these are what I remember.

"Okay, even evil has a place in history, like Hitler, or Bolshevists, or Lenin, or Mao Zedong and so on. Between the Russian and Chinese communist leaders perhaps more than two hundred million country men were exterminated. Their names are all in history books. Applauding them. Yet, their doctrines and their deeds are worth dog manure, not even cow manure because that can be used as fertilizer. I can't believe you still espouse such thinking. I cannot. At your age, I would take vacations and find ways to be more relevant to the human race." My uncle's voice was tamed but unequivocal. As energetic as he was, as vocal as he was, his voice was only two pitches above an average submissive human being. And that was why I adored him -- energetic but civilized, like my father -- at least both had some commonality in temperament. His wife had a lot of voice pull; but she was an angel as well.

"We are talking about isolated cases. Even the Russian communists fought toe to toe against Hitler. You must agree they were relevant. Do not dismiss such undertakings," retorted my grandpa.

"Agreed. So were the Russians, before they were communists; they also defeated Napoleon. Anyone against villains at one time or another will fight and defeat anybody. It does not have to be a communist or socialist."

There was a brief pause; and my uncle decided to take advantage of the moment before any other volley from my grandfather would come his way. By then, at the time of the hot argument, my mother vanished to the kitchen to help my aunt, a decision followed by my sister and my cousin. The other boys were outside playing basketball in the nearby schoolyard. I, grandpa's favorite, listened attentively to the ping-pong match watched by two non-paying fans. It was more like watching a baseball game where there was a pitcher and hitter and vice-versa. At this time, I could do the math that my uncle had three runs and my grandfather had two. Yet, short of any foul ball, my uncle was ready for a grand slam to put the game away. "And, what they have to show for, is that Communism is crumbling and only Socialism a la Great Britain will survive. It does have all the elements of a free world, not subjugated to doctrines, to power of one group with ideas mixed with fear, suspicion and the gun. Gorbachev knows that; and in time Zeng Xiaoping, as well. Just the sheer size of the population, in time, will cause inside out revolution." Another reason I loved my Uncle Frederick was that he knew the world well. He read plenty of the relevant stuff.

"Are you telling me that US policies will prevail, that capitalism is the best form of governing or addressing the economic problems of the masses and for creating an environment of equality? Do you see justice here? Too much corruption in the financial markets? Wall Street commandeers?" My uncle had scored but left men on base, still short of reaching home. I thought my grandfather would erase some runners on the bases. He erased two with his well-positioned argument, but there was still one player on base and my uncle would fill the bases up again.

"All well said." My grandpa smiled; at least he felt he was still in the game and with some batters of his own, with some pull, coming up to bat later. Maybe. "We, as a whole and society per se, do not like that either. And, we'll fight that at the voting booth -- one-man, one vote. Sometimes the votes do not count, but at least we try. Nobody will decide for us or for me or even you. Nobody is above all of us together. My workers can vote the same way I do. I do not tell them whom to vote for. We let their consciences and wits do the voting. We are human beings with rights and freedom of choice. It is not what someone in government tells what is right, what we can eat, whom I associate with. I have freedom to make my own mistakes because there is no one who's above my freedom, no one, and no one can decide my fate for me or my family; I am not a robot, but a human being." Two runners got on base with that testimony.

"The other systems of government also allow people to move up the ranks." My grandfather thought he delivered a strike. It was a ball, not even a close call. My father offered to refill their glasses of wine; they said yes. My father, instead, brought the unfinished bottle of good Chianti. To my father's surprise, both men -- my grandpa and my uncle -- got up. One to the bathroom and the other just to see if his boys had returned from the basketball courts. He had heard some energetic boys' voices and sure enough they had returned and went right back to my cousin Joseph's (the older of all of us) room to play games. I had said I would join them later, which I never did. I wanted to see the whole game outcome and enjoyed the break as if it was in the middle of the seventh inning – a time to stretch your legs and the singing of God Bless America. When all repositioned themselves in their original places, Uncle Fredrick was ready for the grand slam; just needed one more runner on base.

"So, you say in a communist environment and structure people can advance. Honestly? You believe that? How about kissing the behinds of the hierarchy and at the expense of others or everyone being in fear of who is squealing, who's kissing the powers-to-be behinds." I suspected my uncle wanted to say who was kissing whose asses, who was selling their souls at the expense of their neighbors or co-workers who used back-room tactics to advance, who struck fear on whom, and who lived always in an environment of suspicion.

"I'd rather be poor than live in such state of fear. Look at Cuba. As intelligent as they are, they are suffering malnutrition; they have to stay in line for milk and bread, the basic staples. Is Russia supplying them with cars (even lousy cars), computers, telephone systems, with roads, housing? No, they are not. One man, regardless of his intelligence or lack of, controls the lives of over twelve million people. Like a god, just as they'll live forever."

My grandfather wanted to intervene; my uncle said: "you'll have your turn. Let this be my last statement. After all I am your son even if I you do not give a damn about my thinking." My father was not happy with my uncle finally losing his ever-affable manners, or using coarse language to illustrate any point of view.

"Dad, they have nothing to show for -- nothing. America is not perfect, far from it and will never be perfect even if many think it can. But we have freedom to love one another or just not to give a hoot for anybody. What a waste of generations, and talent. I'd rather fight the filthy rich and the crooks, the greedy with my way of living with my friends, and workers and even those with whom I share value at my kids' schools."

I called that relevant and full-of-meat statement, as a two-base hit. And leaving a runner on third and right after a walk to another to first base.

"And that is the problem," said my grandfather, "schools are run by the Catholic religious people. They accept the power of the rich, the power of a government for the wealthy. I don't think they offer free school for the poor." That was only a weak ball four.

My uncle was ready for the grand slam: "Dad, you have never put your feet in any church or schools run by the Catholics. Perhaps you may have been in a hospital run by Catholics, know people that attended Catholic colleges, heard about the hundreds of thousands of soup kitchens that feed the hungry and dressed the poor or even taught side by side with them. They use no guns or fear tactics. They are average good people lending support to many poor people in third world countries and so on. These stories are conveniently ignored, as if they were opium for the masses. They even fought for people's rights along the way, including the black population, or for factory workers in Europe or elsewhere. Catholics did all of that. I knew nothing about them, nothing from you. My kids went there because I wanted a good environment for them. I am happy I finally listened to my wife. My children, your grandchildren, yes grandchildren, have become fine young people, responsible young people because of the water of responsibility and respect they drink at their school. I rarely entered a Catholic church. But I am glad they are there and eventually I may want to drink of that same water. Remember, Dad, that water is not contaminated, has no opium. I've shared my piece and said my peace; it is given to you. I have nothing else to say, for it is just my honest point of view. I am at peace with myself, my family and my country. Sorry, Dad, take it or leave it." Home run, game finished, bottom of the ninth. *That was the way I remembered scoring the game.*

"Well, suit yourself. I'll keep living with my belief. I know no other."

"So be it, Dad. I want nothing but tranquility in your heart." He meant to say soul. He knew better. Besides his eloquence had been restored. My Uncle Frederick was a good orator in college. Yet, with his blue-collar business, he had never had a chance to inspire his friends with speeches. Later in life, his oratorical charm would be displayed in school events. Only later in life, would he display them at my grandfather and father's funerals.

Everybody went home. It was a good Thanksgiving, yet marred by the hot arguments. Certainly, my uncle earned the respect of my father; but hardened my grandfather's resolve. My grandfather, thereafter, rarely would initiate any calls or overtures of any kind to my uncle. My uncle stayed true to his new-found beliefs. One year later, a bombshell, close to an atomic bomb in the family, would strike us. As if to rub my grandfather's nose, my uncle and two of my four cousins -- fourteen and eleven years old -- would be all baptized at Easter Mass in front of a congregation of over five hundred people; and together with eighteen more people, in a prominent corner of the church's holy water's pool, immerse himself in his old, baggy sweatpants. My cousins followed suit. The older cousins had been baptized months after birth; yet were included in the religious rites following baptism. And the applause, I was told later, was beyond anything seen on television. Well, I saw the pictures and two minutes of film, later. We did not attend either the church ceremonies or the happy party staged afterwards for friends and family. My uncle was hurt because his family was not there -- at the event. Yet, he never dwelled on our own mistake; he accepted my father's apology. My father swore that nothing close to events like that one would ever receive a callous or insensitive response. Family was greater than doctrines, greater than blind beliefs, greater than philosophic explanations. My uncle would correctly say to my father. "Reginald, in the end we do not know the whole thing. The world is so complicated and yet fascinating because we have the power to make changes, find the will to do good, and the resolve to make this a better place for all of us." My father would repeat these words. My uncle, at my father's deathbed, thought he did repeat them silently.

By the way, that was one of the very few times that I heard anyone address my father as Reginald. Named Reginald Marx Bingham, my grandfather insisted he be called "Marx;" perhaps after Karl Marx. My grandmother had not allowed that either. By naming me Max, after my father's nickname, everyone got to make their own evaluations and analogies. All would fade away.

∞∞∞∞

After the brief farewell ceremony, I talked for a few moments with my Uncle Frederick. I even asked him about a man I had observed my uncle talking with and then had left shortly after the ashes were scattered in the ocean. I certainly had not invited the stranger to any gathering, including this private one. I suspected my father had other friends I had never met before; yet, a gathering of three dozen people should have triggered some sort of brief and relevant exchanges or simply negligible introductions. My uncle just innocently said that the man had met my father at the hospital during his last days there. "Really? And we never met?" I asked.

"I don't know Max. He praised me for my simple but sincere farewell words to your father."

Max stayed motionless. Uncle Frederick added ... "He projects the image of a nice man and shared very warm comments about your father. I recall him saying that your father died in an unbelievable peace. Who knows? Perhaps he did give the last rites to my brother. When he spoke to me, he said your father was as serene as the calm seawaters we are gazing at now. Some poetry in the statement, I interpreted."

"Strange, he left and never invited himself to know me, my wife or kids. He just chatted with you. Also, strange that I can reconnect with his eyes. I can. I may have seen him at the hospital, too. However, he sported, now, a mustache and longer hair. Not to mention light shaded sun glasses." Max rubbed his cheeks, scratched his nose and then added. "Strange, his eyes could be those of someone who rushed out of dad's hospital room... seconds before dad's last words. Strange!"

"Max, life is strange but beautiful. I was proud of my brother. I admire the way he handled your grandfather. What a peacemaker!"

"Thanks Uncle Frederick. I admire you, too. Besides you are gutsy and above all a joyful person. I wish our lives were more in tune with each other."

"Never mind, Max. Example matters; good deeds matter. You have made our family proud, even if we missed other opportunities to be closer. None of us knows the end of the story. Stay good; stay Max."

I suspected my uncle meant to expand and verbalize more on his thoughts. Yet, respect for what I believed or did not believe, was more important to him. I always loved my Uncle Frederick.

∞∞∞∞∞

I stayed Agnostic and pursued Agnostic information. I even lead a chapter of an Agnostic organization in the city. However, I swore and mandated myself to read all that my father perhaps learned during the last moments of his life. *That strange man … what did he have to teach, to share, to cause my father to experience such a serene and peaceful farewell to life?* Thus, I was determined to learn and discern what was genuine from fake, relevant from posturing, meaningful examples from examples just for show. Or meeting others like my Uncle Frederick -- slowly and logically. I guess I am on the right track. *Be patient Max!*

∞∞∞∞∞

Max, much later in life and on his way to understand the content and meaning of the Bible, the Quran and many teachings of the near and Far Eastern religions or deities, would also come to understand the subtleties of Karl Marx coined phrase -- *Religion is the opium of the masses.* For, Max's involvement and friendship with Fausto and Herbert, would allow him to also interpret that religion could deliver some comfort to those who had little, to those who needed consolation of the heart and soul in addition to the lack of food and respect. In that context, religious comfort also meant stimulation to get up and go, get up and roll up your sleeves; trust in your own marginal sources of power and transform yourself and those around you. Max, thus, was close to defending Karl Marx's potential (unintended) interpretation of the role of religion as a metaphorical medical remedy to pain experienced by those having little or nothing.

Notwithstanding, this poetic metaphor would not win over his grandfather, as it fell so short of the call to arms towards the right to equality. Max thought otherwise, for the means would not justify the ends. Moreover, Max would later come across a very logical answer to the one from which he meant to learn: *Render unto Caesar what belongs to Caesar and unto God what belongs to God. No equality here.*

∞∞∞∞∞

Max's mandate and devotion to learn as much as he could about religions, credos and, above all, the existence of spirituality in a variety of forms, platforms and aspects, helped in some measure. In spite of all this, he admitted that many times all of his research left him more confused, to the point of nearly regretting making such vows. Nevertheless, he set himself ready to develop his plan, to be informed, to understand the whys and set time lines for his achievement. He was not interested in becoming a guru in historical and related religious themes nor in the disparities in Bible interpretations. That was a matter for Catholic minds, for the thousands of protestant denominations or even rabbinical authorities. Putting these divergences aside, he chose a Catholic version of the Bible. Afterall, that version was said to represent the proper bridge from the old to the new testament. Successors of the Hebrew lineage were those Christians that followed Jesus, a Jew himself. If this belief was undeniably fought by Jews, it was hard to fathom that the then Prophets' advanced publicity, two thousand years later, would be still unfulfilled; or that a Messiah was yet to come. Yes, Max was comfortable with his choice of a starting point.

The Quran was a different story that required a different approach. Knowing that it had come to officially exist centuries after

Christianity, also knowing that many but not all of the historical facts from the old testament became guidelines for followers of Islam, Max felt that questions, including his own questions, would abound about their authenticity. His quandary was based in part in the followers' decision to pick-and-choose one genealogy versus another or in the mixing of both genealogies to arrive at the prophet Muhammad's promulgation of a new religion. Of course, he knew he would not achieve expertise, nor did he want to be an arbiter. Therefore, Max chose the Quran for reading only in a limited and cursory manner and scope. And to comfort his decision, the present-day Muslims he read about still lived in two centuries past. *Something is not clicking,* he had concluded. If the numbers of adherents grew, they did by default. The cause could be found in the voids created by the secularization of Christians, or in the inevitable free ticket entrance to countries which were once colonizers. Like saying ... *you conquered and occupied me; now take me with you with all I believe and care. My belief counts; yours does not.*

The Eastern -- whether near East or Far East -- religions, deities, credos, writings were even far more complicated for his brain or perhaps for his lack of patience. If on the one hand he was aware of the value of the inner life, the personal introspection or the meditative aspects of living, on the other hand, this aspect would scare him or freeze his motivation to delve into their existence and related impact in modern society. He did not even mind being wrong because his culture of seeking proof still had much influence on him. Proof carried more weight, more relevancy and thus more appeal than investing more in inner thinking. Another obstacle to the need to know fully about Eastern deities was the perception or later on the conclusion that the Eastern credos were mostly polytheistic driven and centered. Therefore, it did not cut the mustard. With that decision, Max just skimmed the books of Hinduism and Buddhism of India and Confucianism in the far East credos. Research on the edges was good enough for his needs.

In the end, he assured himself to be on the right track in the research, inasmuch as that he had no intentions of becoming an enlightened Agnostic, an enlightened Bible or Scriptures guru, nor the desire to entertain debates with others of diverse backgrounds. He just aimed at being on solid ground towards validating his credence of staying on the fence. His sole purpose, after all, was to prove that both his father's and grandfather's actions and behavior were within the norms of authentic and engaged human beings. His Uncle Frederick's straight-line behavior and exemplary living standards were also worth recognition. Likewise, his wife was happily secular and comfortable; as were his two daughters. One still single and the other married to a make-no-waves, free of clichés or unnecessary-religious-traps young man. He looked at his family package. He was content. Yet, with bugs in his ears.

∞∞∞∞∞

Max confessed years later to his wife, as in a way of justifying a half dozen years of reading and research, that the whole effort had not been easy at all. He further stated that the proof for what he meant to believe was always unreachable. He recalls telling her: *if I do not feel the same way these followers of Jesus feel, there is no point in fighting what I cannot comprehend. Physical or metaphysic facts are outside their thesis.*

For starters, turning the corner on the Old Testament, and finding a straight divine or historical line, or right after Abraham, became a little easier and then messier. Conflict about the early writings was always present. On one hand Max became aware that the Big Book was like a continuous narrative of God's supposedly harsh romance with His people -- a love letter. On the other hand, the choice of one civilization on which to concentrate in the Creator's love, did not compute. It was like concentrating on the template, and the ever experimenting and tweaking the mold, but seldom trying the mold on other civilizations that walked almost side by side. Could he have tried His love letters on others and have seen better results? Or, he did and made no discernable effort to broadcast the outcomes. Most likely He had his eye on a radical plan a few millenniums down the road. Or, his plan *B*. Certainly, it was abundantly understood and proved that His hand was on other civilizations that were marching to a specific rhythm of their own drums and making some sort of progressive noise for themselves. Whether it was the Stonehenge civilization, the Incas, Asiatic examples, or the pyramids of Egypt, what supposedly mattered was the chosen people -- the Hebrews. Thus, a question mark was always present.

Max felt relieved when his learning journey reached the New Testament. He came to be enamored of Jesus Christ and everything that related to him. Everything about Jesus was relevant; even ambiguity was always explained. Max actually admired a man that harnessed that much intellect, candor, love, pull and motivation to cause acceptance of (ugly) death as a worthwhile cause. *I told you it would not be easy following me;* that was a phrase Max remembered so well. In the end, he wished he would have understood that magic of influencing sad and poignant outcomes as being acceptable rewards. *Gosh, almost three hundred years of martyrs or the so-called* followers of Jesus not rejecting him, his teachings and promises of invisible-after-death rewards. He concluded in his confessions to his wife: "Katheryn, I do not possess this faith nor do I seek to comprehend this phenomenon. I guess you do not as well. Or perhaps one day we'll find the answer. Who knows?

6

The professor and his students

Meeting preparation

Science without religion is lame
Religion without science is blind
-----Einstein

Elvera checked her smart phone to confirm her driving route. Highway 580 was the most logical and preferred itinerary. She got two readings -- 580 had an accident and 880, with its usual large number of trucks, had been impacted by a lane closure due to construction. Besides, in order to get to 880, one needed the 238 connector. This, by historic data, was always clogged until noon. The phone GPS listed another choice -- Crow Canyon Road to 680 and then 24 West to connect with 580. The driving time of this choice, normally double the direct 580 freeway, was about the same -- forty-five minutes. Instead of getting annoyed, Elvera accepted the delay as she had left the house early. She thought wisely and recaptured the *details that placed her and her partners in the mission, on the trail of a University of the Bay Area professor. Like her friends, she thought that the professor must have been part of a panel at an earlier conference. Now, that the group was bound to meet Professor Eichelberger for the project's final instructions, it was important to flash back to how they met. Forty-five minutes and small change was what it took for her to firm all the details in her mind.*

As she drove, Elvera smiled at times, chuckled at others when some of the scenes, and in part the ones when her Walter took almost center stage, made everyone laugh. Yes, Walter was good at that. And their friends loved it, too.

∞∞∞∞∞

As they waited for the good-byes, a tall gentleman, casual but nicely dressed in good but somewhat wrinkled grey pants, in a collared light blue shirt and a navy-blue cardigan, approached their table. He was accompanied by another gentleman whom he dismissed with a "I'll talk to you later." From a sitting position, all looked up to the gentleman, as he was tall.

"Pardon me for interrupting your friendly chat." *How could he tell? Was he listening?* Mumbled Walter. "I could not help but listen to parts of your rich dialogue. Almost like eavesdropping. I apologize, very rich and intriguing conversation, indeed." *The guy is a bull-shitter,* continued Walter's mumbling.

"What can we do for you?" asked Herbert.

"My name is Joachim Eichelberger. My acquaintances call me Jake. I am a professor next door, at the University of the Bay Area.

Can I impose on your time for a mere minute and ask you a couple of questions, or even make you a proposition?"

As two of the five looked at their watches, Professor Eichelberger hesitated a moment and said: "I suspect you had a long morning, coupled with the debriefing luncheon. Here is my business card." Actually, the professor fished for several. "It would be very kind of you to give me a call about my request. My students and I would be ever grateful for your opinions."

Max looked the others in the eyes and said. "It is okay. If it is just a minute, we can oblige and learn what you have in mind. Let me get a chair for you." Max pulled another chair from next to the table where the professor had just finished his meal and offered it to him. "We can be brief but no need for you to stay standing. Go ahead, finish your question. By the way, my name is Max, Max Bingham."

"And you Madam? I am sorry for not asking you to introduce yourselves. I did not want to bother you as I did."

"Oh, not a problem. My name is Elvera Betancourt." Elvera, although finished with her introduction, grinned innocently.

The professor hesitated with the next introduction. Instead he asked "anything wrong, Mrs. Betancourt?"

"Yes and no; or no and yes. Your name sounds familiar. We attended a short conference a couple of months ago and I swear your name was mentioned. I'm sorry."

"You are absolutely correct; you have a great memory. In fact, I did organize the conference, invited credible guests and enticed many to come. Like you, you must have heard my name but never saw me."

All delivered their individual smiles more as curiosity and the professor added: "I had a bad infection on my right eye -- the best of the two -- and could not come. Pain and a large patch around my eye would not have added value to the conference. Wrong time and environment to gather some sort of pity. Anyway, I understand it went well, and I am glad that you also attended the presentation."

All nodded politely. The professor, now stimulated, turned to Walter. "Oh, it's my turn? I am this lady's husband, and her servant." All broke in laughter; any vestige of ice had just been melted.

The two men in their mission of being close to God introduced themselves. And, to the surprise of the professor, both revealed what they did for a living. For the professor, the relevancy of the potential proposition climbed up a notch in importance. At least the professor thought so, and proceeded to explain the mission he had for his graduate students in philosophy.

"I think we can do that. However, we need to consult with each other in some manner, and come back to you for a conversation before the project." Looking to the others for help and getting positive nods, Max finished the commitment. "Vera will communicate with you about a date and place. Remember, you cited six of us to match six of your students. Is that right?"

"Yes, it is. For various reasons and more. I know … the more is to create the best harmony of thoughts together. And you are a perfect fit, I am certain of that."

"Wait, wait. I nodded but did not say my peace," asserted Walter. "I am not in the same league as you guys are. I have no college education or profess the knowledge you have. This needs to be thought over."

"Walt is a game player, but has his logical reservations. Yet, we shall see." declared Elvera. Then added: "there is no obstacle. If we participate, it will be six players; I suppose my husband will be included. Don't worry professor."

"That would be great, for he has humor. Indeed, I am excited with the possibilities, for you represent a very diversified sample of humanity. Of course, your friend Sam, the one you were investing time in conversation, would be a winner, too."

"We well know that. But he will be a no go. That is for sure."

"Please wait a minute you all." Walter spoke again, but this time with some sort of authority. "Let's wait more than a minute and learn some opening details. At least for me to learn if my wife and I will have a duel this afternoon -- on the road or at home." Intellectual laughter came to the table one more time. "What is it about your need for our input? Can we do this Max? Ask a few questions? That you declared Vera the go-to person, is fine. She's always looking for assignments. Can we do this people? Get some questions answered?"

Max said: "Yes, we can." Now, looking at his watch and turning to the professor, he added: "Granted that each one of us has other things to do; however, Walt is right. All the important protagonists are here; so, some little but crucial details can be dealt with now. Professor, can we learn about your project in just a few minutes?"

"Of course, I can. I am sorry again, for imposing on your generosity. Let me see. First, my students already have majors, whether in psychology, divinity and even theology. However, they are pursuing their masters in philosophy. I have three groups researching material for their exams. We all target places, history, people, situations, events to collect deserving material. We do our homework. However, you folks come across as a gift. The diversity of your backgrounds, I assume, and what I perceive as your seriousness of purpose is unequal in any level. You are real. Hence, the importance of interviewing and gaining authentic knowledge in a unique and relevant model. Sorry for this mouthful. For instance, you, Max. What do you do?"

"I am an insurance broker."

"And you, Madam?"

Elvera said she was a retired Regional Communications Executive; Mancini and Hawkins reiterated what they had stated before, and Walter said he was in HVAC business, now semi-retired.

"Sorry for asking ...HVAC ... but what is that?"

"Also sorry for being a *Smart as ... Alec.* My business is in heating, air-conditioning and related mechanic and plumbing work."

"Well, wow -- a self-made man. I am so elated to meet you, Walt."

"Pardon me, but I am not what your think; for these self-proclaimed, *pardon my French.* ... piece of dung, were never self-made. Many, many people helped me along the way. I got help and advice; I got vendors bailing me out time-and-time-again, very dedicated employees; and above all a wife who inspired me, supported me when business was not good enough to pay me a decent salary. Oh, yah, even cared to sleep with me in bed." The last truth floored the whole group, again.

"Sorry, for laughing too, Walt. But you are so colorful; you are rich in zingers, full of truth. And thanks for being so candid, so natural. This means you do not believe that people succeed without help from others."

"Certainly, this is one of my pet-peeves. And we have one in the White House that proclaims to be a self-made guy; pounding his chest as the star of self-made dung. My friends here know a little bit about me. I am proud to know them because this adds to what I am."

Walter took a breather and concluded: "not to waste any more time, and this is about self-made folks. All of us, real human beings got help all the way from the cradle to what we are now. Many people helped people to succeed. But I told you that. My creed -- people help people to succeed or others cheat people to succeed. One or the other -- I rest my case."

"Wow, wow, Mr. Betancourt. This is a first for me. Not only are you eloquent but also thought and tongue courageous." The professor took a pause and finished: "Thanks folks. No need for more details. You are all winners and recipients of mutual, reciprocal help. I will remember that."

"Thanks, Walt. I did not expect a lecture on a very dear theme," said Elvera. "Now I have to do my job. And that is to communicate with you, Professor Eichelberger. I will call in days to learn the rest."

"Please, please call me Jake. And with no irony of any kind, I am so grateful for this chat. Walt, make an effort to participate. I hate to use the phrase *you are a winner*; yet, you all complement each other so well. Unequivocally, my students and I are bound to achieve more success because of you." Now turning to Elvera, he said: "I will wait for your call, right?"

"Right it is." concluded Elvera.

∞∞∞∞∞

"My Lord, you did not have to be so impulsive on your reaction to the professor's praise. I know you are as truthful as a raw egg -- full of protein and ready to be cooked in a variety of ways and flavors. Yet, accepting praise is a virtue," declared Elvera as they took the road home. She was ambivalent about her criticism of Walter; but felt the time was ripe for the certain duel Walter had alluded to earlier. She knew, from few "pow-wows" before, that Walter could drive, concentrate on the road and then admit he should be more civilized. She also knew, as her friends claimed, that Walter was the most charismatic friend to have. She was beyond being proud. She drank from Walter's raw wisdom and unconditional love.

"I am sorry! You are right. I had two chances to shut up, but let my tongue take over without getting help from my brain. Well, I live with that and then regret and then say *what the heck!*" He giggled, drove more, looked at Elvera and stayed silent. Elvera thought about Walter's usual confession -- repent and matter-of-fact posture. Additionally, he would say -- *it is the way God made me. In your constant prayers, ask Him to fix my habits.* And she knew better than to challenge the truth as raw and pure as what her Walt would deliver.

"I understand and live with it with some consternation and then unbelievable pride. What you said about this self-made thing is true. The professor immediately fell in love with such spontaneity. He did, for he must have few of these reactions in life. I have no idea about his politics; however, he could be a liberal type; disfranchised of the Right's rhetorical pontifications."

"Wow! Are you preparing a speech to your typical audience? Displaying the fancy vocabulary? Talk my language, darling. Talk my lingo," retorted Walter with smart giggling.

"In fact, I was. And I plan to utilize some of what you said. It is colorful, like the professor said. I bet he interacts with the fine philosophical types. He must always deal with science and themes above our heads. Yes, I was. Now, look back at what you said and at his reaction. Saying the correct things is not always right. Granted, your reaction was magnanimous..."

"Stop Elvera. Once again you used an intellectually rich word -- magnan...imous. Let me repeat ... magnanimous ... tough for my tongue. Let's be serious -- you are not going to rehearse a speech now. Are you?" reacted Walter.

"No speech over here. And you are right; let's get out of this thing. My take is that you displayed the Walter I know, and the poor professor was in love with it. And you just admitted you could have been better. Therefore, case closed. Now, you are going to participate in the project; if it goes forward. Can I count on you?"

"Of course, I will. When was the last time I said I love you and did not?"

"Even in joking you deliver love notes," added Elvera.

"Good; besides I always make some noise but then relent. However, it depends when I have my golf tournaments."

"I know, I will respect them. Peace!"

"Thanks, Vera, for being my girlfriend!"

She bounced her head, smiled at him and with glowing eyes said: "you fool; I love you more!"

∞∞∞∞∞

At the pre-conference project meeting, the professor, besides wanting to recollect the impromptu meeting they had held three weeks prior, wanted to piggy back on Walt's credence that everybody needs help, everybody gets help to succeed. Likewise, the reverse -- lousy results -- stem from bad help, bad beginnings.

Children from some welfare parents tend to become welfare recipients -- systemic bad following, like friends who take drugs. In other words -- bad starts from family, community conditions, and bad luck cause people to be bad or do bad things. Bad outcomes are not exclusive to one person alone. It potentially involves environments, culture, circumstances, genes and a whole assortment of causes that separate humans from other humans. Whether he was a believer of cosmic sources, of elements rarely discussed in schools, places of work, or of the absence of divine intervention, he was aware of the human conditions, anxieties, potential, fulfillment and achievement.

He just cared for his students to be enlightened by all that was available from the side of science or the side of spirituality. Or the essence that God existed before and now -- in their lives. He also knew that the majority of the whole world was ignorant of the essential facts; never questioning the teachings of so many and always at odds with preachers or vendors of the easy solutions. He knew the immense schools of thought throughout the ages offered opinions that were directed at the scientists themselves rather than at the multitude of human beings -- the very, absolute vast majority of humanity. He, time and again, would be confronted with the answers and questions of the pragmatists -- why worry or pay attention to your clever discoveries if none bring food to the table or shelter over my head. Why? What do you know about suffering? Or do you care about it if there is no life after death? Why? If there is nothing after the now, what good is it to hope for something you fail to comprehend? If your theories cannot fix the fixable, why invest time in learning more, in reading more, or ... *he would later on state to himself* ... gamble that he would be wrong, dead wrong and perhaps miserable. At least, he would recognize, that *hope* was a great intangible. Yet, hope was not a word in his repertoire. Hope, like love, like inner peace, was not in the province of the intellectual cosmic background. Nevertheless, he wanted his students, now more academically prepared, to discern for themselves. This included exploring the inner feelings, the emotions of the spirit. Yes, why not? -- emotions of the heart and soul.

Well, he was no longer an iconoclast of sorts; far from the young teacher and idealistic philosopher. In less than a year he would retire and devote more time to and exploring areas he had bypassed before. No wonder that Walter's impromptu reactions rang true in his mind. Too much raw honesty could be explored. What differentiated Walter's raw reactions from intellectual or the rhetorical ones, were not and could not be easily explained by the simple expression or claim "it depends" -- where you are and live, came from or learned. The professor thought, in the form of a question, that when he died and Walter died, what would the world have gained? How better had it turned out? Or better in what? What were their individual and separate legacies? Were measurable and measured legacies important? Particularly, if after death, nothing would be important within the terms they were familiar with. What would these measures be? The measures of the rich and the poor? By the power or subservience? By the enlightened or prophetic? He had more questions now than when he was very young or even naïve. He pondered. He pondered.

∞∞∞∞∞

Elvera arrived separately and not as early as she planned. Max had done the same for he also had bad traffic. One lived in Castro Valley and the other in Orinda. Stretching, but they could have car-pooled together but did not. The other two from San Francisco would ordinarily take BART and find their way to rendezvous points. Normally these encounters would be near BART stations in downtown Oakland, and then, receive rides from the others who drove. This time, Fausto and Herbert would meet at the University's BART station -- located a few minutes from the campus. As pre-arranged, Herbert waited for Fausto and both directed themselves to the campus.

"Was it difficult to find this conference room?" asked the professor in a concerned mode.

"Oh, no. Not for me," said Elvera. "Once I mentioned your name and where to meet you, I was guided with no problems." Max did the same.

Elvera found the professor's inquiry and concern somewhat odd and then stated: "This is a big and very spread-out campus; however, I hope you have not advertised our participation in your project. I hope not. It appeared the guide knew all about where to meet you and the subject matter."

Before the professor answered the question, Herbert and Fausto showed up. The professor asked the same question: "How did you do? Difficult to get here?"

"None at all. Were we supposed to get lost?" asked Fausto.

"Well, Jake, can you fill me in?" asked Elvera.

The professor, taken a bit off-guard and turning to Herbert and Fausto, replied, "Vera thinks the whole world here knows about the project and who participates."

"So?!" reacted Herbert.

"The students, in this part of the campus, know there is a surprise outcome from this research. That is all. Of course, they are free to share info on what they know. But none else from me. Trust me."

"Good. I feel relaxed," retorted Elvera.

"You should now find a seat, and we shall begin once I know what I can offer you -- coffee, tea or water. I hope after our chat you can join me for lunch in our semi-private cafeteria." Elvera said she would take tea; Max and Hebert said coffee and Fausto just plain water.

Showing three neat packages of documents, the professor just enumerated them — the participants' simple and limited information, the guidelines and questionnaires themselves. As the student that guided them brought the drinks and a cookie tray, the professor started the meeting.

"Once again I thank you for helping my students on this project. I suspect you value your participation, otherwise, you would individually and collectively find honest excuses to pass this chance. And like Walt said, people need people to cause success to be achieved." The others just froze their attention. "I am not saying this just as a formality; it is pure honesty. By the way I would not mind rewinding the last statements from Walt. Can we do this, Vera?"

"I cannot remember every joke he shared; none worthy of a project like the one you have in hand. Certainly, Walt would be annoyed. He would say it in a different tone and language which I will not repeat." Laughter from the previous short encounter returned. Elvera continued, "like I said, if we dwelt too much time on this issue, he would bolt out of this meeting."

The others said little other than frowning with the possibility of returning to the scene of the encounter. Elvera sipped some tea, and continued. "Accept Walt's regrets that seemed like he resented your praise. That is the way he is. He wants to be appreciated on his terms -- take it, enjoy it; but move on, make no comments."

"That is fair. I guess most people of good will and standing want the same. Go on," said the professor.

"So, Walt admitted his roughness; not so, but he claimed his mouth or tongue was ahead of his brain. Like when he guesses that his brain caught the tongue, his tongue is in the second stage. Do you know what I mean?"

They all let their smiles, giggles, their nods as proof they did. Elvera continued. "For instance, the other day after an event at the Rotary club, Walt, as we returned home, made a comment I had never heard him make before."

"The Rotarians, like the Kiwanis, or the Lions or Breakfast clubs or SIRS, or many others, all have their protocol and rituals." The professor was a member of none cited but remembered these well on two occasions in his early teaching career; as a guest speaker. He motioned Elvera to continue.

"So, we know the format, the rituals, etc. Walt must have followed the culture or repeated the words zillions of times, sang the songs like 'God Bless America' and or said the "Pledge of Allegiance.' You name it. However, after this dinner he took issue with the 'Pledge of Allegiance.'"

Seeing some doubt on the faces of her listeners she concluded: "I pledge Allegiance to the flag... blah, blah, one nation under God with ... blah, blah... and with liberty and justice for all. As we drove home, the best venue for us to talk, he made a pointed comment which hit me in my mind and heart. The words that resonated to or with him then, and then to me, were about *Justice for all*."

"How come?" said Max.

"Max, you have known us for a few years. Not long but enough for one to disclose our alliances, our hobbies, our politics. Remember, even today he keeps politics off the table. Including with his buddies at golf clubs. He directs conversations to his golf scores, the Raiders; (he calls them the Traitors), the A's; the Cal Bears; (our daughter studied there). But he pushes out conversations on politics."

"Do you and Walt talk politics? Like just the two of you!?" ventured Herbert.

"We do," said Elvera. We do all the time. I am more progressive and Walt is in the middle of the road -- a moderate Democrat. We talk issues all the time; policies on quick fixes that later on turn into nightmares, into blame games, and hypocritical accusations mostly on 'it was this party's fault.' Blame game and blame game."

"Then!?" pushed Max.

"Then, on our drive home from the Rotarians event in Sacramento -- a longer than normal ride -- he asks 'When was the Pledge of Allegiance written or started being used in these meetings or other patriotic functions? Can you tell me when?' I said I suppose it was in the mid - 20th Century or thereabouts. Well, then I fumbled and said: I recall reading that it had been recited in some form at the end of the nineteenth century; but modified in the fifties."

"Walt asked then 'did we still have segregation at that time, in the mid-nineteen fifties?' I said I was positive we still had official segregation because the Civil Rights Act was only passed during the early sixties. If that was what he meant.

"Then he said and quoted, 'liberty and justice for all.' Can you see, Vera? "All?!'"

"We stayed quiet for a while and then he gave me the punch line: 'All, meaning just for the white boy -- liberty and justice for the *white boy, the Anglo-Saxon*?! I understood his message. I understood Walt's message!"

"And what do you do now? Did this fact modify your views of politics, social justice, or even racism of some form?"

"No, professor, no. I am not an activist. But I speak my mind when the situation calls for it. I take stands, positions in an unequivocal manner and when I find the theme appropriate. We have to. Otherwise our progress towards a more equitable society slips through our hands and betrays the trust others placed in us."

"And about Walt?" asked the professor again.

"No. Like me, he is not an activist. He does not have this in his DNA. But he speaks his mind, and some of his friends resent it. And he replies with his colorful language, like waterfront lingo. And, I blush and love him more."

They all laughed and became ready for the purpose of the professor and his students' project.

∞∞∞∞∞

"Thanks Vera. I hope Walt comes to the conference."

"Oh, he'll come. And by the way, the friend of mine I thought would fit well, will also come. She just returned from a long trip -- nine months -- through Africa and some Far-East countries. She writes essays for some research firms and for herself. In time, she'll have her own book. I am happy for us that she will come."

"That's good. Now here are the profiles for all who participate on the project. Each profile has just four pages. The first -- the front -- is the project name. Yeah, yeah; you do not like it... **God does not exist!** ... I thought so. It also has a clever sub-title -- '**So what?**'. Next is the page of simple information about yourselves -- very few lines limited in details."

"I like the 'So what?' very clever and with open room for debate." Said Herbert.

"Indeed, indeed it was the purpose -- anger some people and then elicit rebuttal. That is the purpose," added the professor.

"You, philosophers, love the ironies," rebutted Herbert.

After the brief philosophic exchange, the guests used their own set and followed the professor's explanation. "On the name line ...

only the first name is required; on the gender line, male or female; or age -- just the approximate age. Example -- Fifty plus or sixty plus or if close to seventy, seventy minus. Yes, it seems a funny approach. Psychology, my friends; university style."

"On profession, do you imply the formal explanation? Or, a generic one will suffice?" asked Max.

"Generic is fine," said the professor. "In your case, I would indicate *Casualty and Industrial Insurance Broker.*"

"For Walt I would write *'self, Heating and Air Conditioning services.'* For you, Fausto and Herbert I would indicate member of the clergy. And for your friend, Vera, write down *freelance* researcher. Or something to that effect."

"The other pages have barely a few lines but enormous amounts of space. How would you want us to answer these? Narrative, essay type?"

"Whatever you wish to include, Max." Smiling the professor added, "If you need more space add other sheets of paper."

Getting some frowning and shades of sarcasm, the professor added: "Seriously, I would not bother with too much detail. Remember you are not in school. And, you are doing us a favor; no unnecessary struggle here. It is basically some info where the students will establish a physical or intellectual image of yourselves. Later on, your smiles, your body language, your voice emphasis will trick, innocently trick them. Like in life, until you know a person more, you can never assume you know someone well."

He continued: "There are six students and each one will have a question -- one only -- for each one of you. So, we will have thirty-six individual and different questions and answers. Some similarities in the questions; but none identical."

"It sounds scientific and broad in scope," replied Elvera.

"You nailed it correctly, Vera. Once we compile the info, the answers will be placed in various categories. Yet, your own answers during the questions and answers session will reveal information that is uniquely valuable. It will convey your emotion, your knowledge and above all the amount of authenticity gleaned from your convictions. We are talking about you, real people, with real experiences, almost identical but not necessarily rendering knowledge based on beliefs or experience as opposed to fiction."

"What do you mean by that?" asked Fausto.

"Fausto, you are an agent of God who practices works of support, inspires people to see divinity as the almost absolute means of living, or addressing day-to-day issues, needs, aspirations. Or, your views may be mixed with doubt, other possibilities. However, from the get go, I see all of you as very independent thinkers, and evaluators of what you do and do not know. You are a complete package not influenced by some theoretical force. Do you understand me? I mean, all of you?"

Fausto was still configuring the professor's mixed description as a form of explaining what the students were aiming to learn. The professor understood Fausto's facial expression and added: "Fausto, you know, the students minds and ages will dictate questions that not only reveal their curiosity but also their boldness. They may even try to present themselves as astute students, as visionaries of some kind. You know better and then you will put them in their spots in a credible way. Avoid pontificating in some manner. However, your collective participation is different, for it involves six proven, inherently unique worlds."

"I understand, thanks." Replied Fausto Mancini.

"What you are doing is magnificent. But I do not need to tell you this. You are the product of earth's existence; you are the continuity of the world's presence -- whatever notion one may have." added the professor with the intent of no-pontificating but emphasizing and assuring the value of the partnership between them and his students.

He continued: "They will read your answers. Then they will discern the intent and meaning of collaboration. Then, they will add the trust implicitly set and conveyed in your answers. This will not make or break their preparation for their thesis. For, like I said before, they already have much material to assist them with their final conclusions. However, your sharing will reinforce their own theories or reveal weaknesses in their own gathered material -- some fact from fiction. This is life. This is basically one important step in many where relevancy will impact their life; how they will choose to conduct it and fulfill their professional aspirations. This is my take ..."

All felt the professor wanted to convey and mix his own beliefs. They let him in... "I have lived my life and have much more to live. And in this business, not in terms of money, but pursuing what is yet to be known, I have done what I could. However, my students are at best having a taste of what they will deliver on the next thirty or forty years of their lives. This is the beginning of their impact; I preach relevant impact on the planet. So, your part will be a test. Because you are part of the world that has been already explored and revealed."

"I, for one, get your message and I am willing to play in this game of real life, impart what can be relevantly imparted." Intervened Elvera.

"This is all I trust you will deliver. Sorry, I know you will. And my life will be better. For instance, we are creatures of change and, by that, I mean we impart what we believe and let the rest take care of itself. I am, if one can put labels, an Agnostic a la Einstein or closer to a Bertrand Russell. By, the way, do you know that there wasn't such category as Agnostic before Bertrand Russell's famous speech?"

"It depends on which side you were. I have learned from other sources that there was no such thing. People, after listening to him and his debates with the likes of G.K. Chesterton and others coined the name of Agnosticism. So, Bertrand by his very speech, became the founder of Agnosticism." retorted Herbert.

"Well, Chesterton was more than a pragmatic philosopher. He was the only one, in my view, that could debate with Russell and not feel an ounce of bitterness. Like saying … living my life believing in what I know and then finding out I was wrong is not a bad thing. At least I left a trail of good will for others to chase the final answer," affirmed Elvera.

"Did he say this that way? Are you quoting G.K.'s words?"

"No, I am not, professor. But that is what I interpreted he said. Remember he was a man of multiple talents and activities. His life, as a whole, research and life on the stage, left us an enormous legacy. In that league, but much later, I can include C.S. Lewis."

"All credible figures. Sometimes opposites of one another. Yet," continued the professor, "C. S. Lewis was more a lay theologian than a philosopher."

He then added, "I love what we're talking now and should add more of what we know to the pot, before we go to lunch; my treat at the cafeteria; not a bad one for a school. Would you accept my invitation?"

No one committed and then the professor said "you will decide later, like in half an hour. Unless you prefer your usual places to eat on this side of the Bay."

The four, instinctively, held their preferences back (undisclosed) and let the professor continue. "Here is what I can add now. These students I am responsible for, range from twenty-four to thirty years of age. All of them already know what they want to do in life. Some are already doing superb things in life. I also sense that a few will be heard of, later in life. Of my thirty some students, one or two, in time will teach in this institution of learning. They are that good. So, all of them have experience, but are still shy of your own experience. Don't worry; have no mercy on them, be factual and add your other variables in your life; like love, feelings, pain, joy, happiness. I do not know it all. Einstein did not know it all. I know, I know … an Agnostic talking bravely about love and these mysterious or intangible feelings! Go ahead send me to jail." The professor smiled broadly as he said that and then continued.

"They have all read about the most celebrated or relevant and well-regarded philosophers. They have read from Plato, Aristotle, from Pantheists; from Aquinas, Augustine." He stopped, then resumed. "Granted, Augustine is not thought of as being a philosopher in the same league as the others. However, everyone loves Augustine. Smart as he was, his life had so much in common with us. His *Confessions* and *City of God* put him miles apart from other known philosophers of his time. Again, let me use the word authentic. Augustine read and valued the Greek philosophers. That, in itself, allows students to call his works credible."

Fausto and Herbert, as they dissected their views later, thought that the professor had a weakness for St. Augustine.

The professor regrouped his thoughts and added: "Therefore, they read everything and more. And those students that have no religion affiliation or affinity admire Jesus Christ. They all conclude that, if Jesus were undressed of spiritual and divine clothes, Jesus would be and is the most credible philosopher and human example of all times. No one comes close. Not Gandhi, not Mother Teresa, not even Francis de Assisi. One of my students even claimed that Jesus taught the world about the best business practices. Do not hoard money unnecessarily, but treat people, subordinates well and get the best out of them."

"Do you believe that?" asked Max.

"At first, I paused and told my student we would talk later; then he floored me with this example: 'Who could make use of all human beings? Like none left behind? Not one.' There is no economist in the planet that can challenge that thinking and approach. From my point of view, I am a believer. Not too fast! There is much we do not know yet."

"And what was your final answer?" asked Max.

"I gave him an 'A' and surrendered to the fact that he would be a good Christian philosopher. One that would challenge my throne. That was all I said to him."

∞∞∞∞∞

All decided to accept the professor's now mild and polite invitation to have a meal at the cafeteria. More exchanges followed the ones they had before at the professor's teaching room. Although the cafeteria provided no coziness similar to the teaching room, they were free to let their minds validate their verbalized thoughts and opinions. Max's vast amount of reading of the Bible, the Koran and enlightenments from the Eastern culture, impressed the professor to the point of causing Max to explain the purpose of such mission. Receiving the basis for such research the professor asked where Max stood on the matter of God's existence or the planet's creation. Max had shrewdly explained that his mission was yet to be finished. The more he mingled with folks possessing other views and beliefs, the more fun and personal joy he experienced.

"Professor, the very fact that I am ambivalent, is the answer to my slow feet on accepting one or the other belief. Feelings, professor; feelings. One cannot push away these from our everyday life. And the concepts of things happening by chance are far from feelings of love, caring, from wanting to add value, and making the world better. Just this desire to make the planet better separates the cold, obtuse, notion that the 'by chance' has pull, nurtures feelings."

"Well," said the professor, "animals also possess some sort of feelings. Nothing in the same platform as humans. Yet, they help one another, defend and protect one another, feed one another during the progressive years of their lives and so on. And, like humans, fight for territory very ferociously."

"All good, but falling short of the human brain, the machine that feeds everything that happens to us."

The professor meant to put an end, polite and logic end to the exchanges, particularly coming from someone he came to respect and share the same ideology -- Agnosticism. "Max, I buy everything you said. Yet, we need another environment for our discussions. Do you want to come to class and discuss philosophy with me and my students?"

"I know you are saying this in jest and perhaps I could validate your position or your status. Let's instead see how your students will fare with us."

"I was smiling but serious. You can come because you appear credible. You run your own Agnostic club in the Bay Area."

"How do you know that?" asked Max.

"Like all of you do: I Googled Agnostic clubs in the Bay Area."

All became numbed; the professor continued: "About the students ... don't bet on an exchange like this one we are having. Even though our enlightened clergymen have stayed somewhat quiet; relinquishing their religious power to our clever layperson here." He stopped and then resumed. "How do we do this thing politically correct? Laywoman, layperson, lay-lady?" They all laughed.

"You can be funny; not a la Walt, but funny," intervened Elvera. "And this is all part of the creative authority, like smiling and telling zingers."

"Now you are pushing some buttons," retorted the professor. Turning to the three men he threw a question: "What do you say 'spiritually endowed' friends?"

"She can do well and hold her own. She is a real package, professor," said Fausto. "Deferring to her is a privilege."

"Well, thanks for coming. Having flexibility on your schedules helps, too. I assure you will not regret what you do."

"We well know this. We help others that really need our help, too." Finished Herbert.

∞∞∞∞∞

They all said their good-byes and left for their destinations back home. Before that and as they gathered at the yard around the cafeteria building, all confirmed that they had a lucrative meeting, knew what they had to do to answer the questionnaires, and agreed to be equal to the task: no more nor less than -- adding value to the students mandates or distracting them from their pursuits of truth. Elvera and Max went to the parking garage where their parking tickets had been validated by the professor, whereas the two agents of God walked their way back to the train station.

"Fausto, I admit the professor's project has much substance and it will help his students deliver the goods; i.e., build their own thesis credibly and with some juice." Fausto smiled at Herbert's choice of flavorful words. "Likewise, Max was unbelievably coherent. His unassuming positions were enlightening though. I wish some of my congregants were here to hear good, soul searching and open-minded human beings. Rather than stuck-on-the-sand minds."

"I think in the same way. We, many in the Catholic church, are equally so vehemently stubborn in their and our ways."

"Do you fight this? Collectively or one-to-one?"

"Not really. It is always case by case. Or touching the matter on the periphery."

With their tamed but proven enthusiasm on the conversation, like a debriefing thing, both got lost or took the wrong way towards the train station. They stopped, reevaluated their position and veered back and westbound. Fausto laughed and said, "can we surmise that there was ecumenism on this meeting today? Like everyone respecting each other's position without any sign of condescension or pontification? Could this meeting have been held before Vatican II? Could it, Herb?"

"I don't know but doubt it would be as civilized and fluid as this one. In fact, it would stop in its tracks very quickly. I was not one to get impressed with Vatican II. However, it began the process of a potential reconciliation. We, in our side, felt it was more an internal house cleaning of ideas and formalities on the part of the Catholics. For instance, your Pope John ... twenty-third? Was it, Fausto?" Fausto confirmed the pope's name. "He changed, from what I read, your pomposity, the outside layers, the unnecessary, the show, the rigidity of dogmas. But the changes were too small to make an impact on our conclusions about the Catholic Church. Do you agree with my thinking?"

"I do, I do. I was a kid, still in grammar school when my parents spoke of this matter at the dinner table. My mother had some doubts. My father was excited for the church and the rituals would be more relevant and near the congregants. He even gave the example that Jesus always was in communion with the disciples, never turning his back to them. My father was happy with the changes; but feared for how long the old guard would tolerate Pope John's changes. The Curia still held much power."

"I can see, Fausto. That could have been the beginning for the Catholic Church in recognizing that the Reformation was over. Almost five centuries would have been enough to understand that the Church failed; and, by failing, instigated others to move away from you. Don't you think so?"

"Again, I do. Granted that Martin, unlike other great Christians of the era or before, like Francis and company, was so opinionated and stubborn. John Calvin was actually very mean, very mean and vindictive," Fausto added as if to justify the Pope's misgivings.

"Okay," affirmed Herbert. "Let's just say that everyone was up to no good, including some popes."

"No problem with that. But let me add another one that got the religious world even more in disarray." Herbert just glanced at Fausto and Fausto continued: "For instance, King Henry VIII was no exception. And just because he wanted another wife. My Lord."

"Not just divorcing once; but four more times," said Herbert.

"He had a good lawyer to defend his actions… Cromwell? I remember … Thomas Cromwell. As opposed to another good

Christian named Thomas -- Thomas Moore." Fausto stopped and Herbert waved him to go on. "Well, King Henry, like the others, started another religion; oh my God. What a mess!" Fausto concluded but not before acknowledging that Martin Luther must have had enough; that something had to give.

"Good point. Much was going wrong with the Catholic Church leaders at that time. Most of their own doing," said Herbert.

"In my case, I have been so eager to see more changes, more substantial changes in areas besides the Vatican Bank, the overwhelming amount of administrative areas, bureaucracy."

"That is the price of being global in all matters; too much bureaucracy in the Catholic Church! Agree?" finished Herbert.

Fausto indicated that he agreed. Herbert added. "You guys have to do more. Having more than two thousand official religions in California means that Vatican II is still a little far. No justification for such thing."

"Right on. Like now, you and I, walking together and sharing our common goal of following Jesus. That is all that matters. Ecumenism at its best. We must extend this environment to others. Yet, even if we have a long way to go, it will not take five hundred years since Martin Luther and John Calvin's reformation. You are right, Herb."

"Let's get in. I will read my morning prayer and you -- your breviary. Is that it?"

"Yes, it is. But, instead, I will read from Pope Francis. His actions are carbon copies of Vatican II. And many times, he is not understood in our Church."

"Good boy, Francis -- a repeat of John XXIII."

"You got it."

They got to San Francisco and made their way towards their comfort zones.

7

After the students' thesis project

Revisiting Reformation
Keeping the Church honest

You cannot do kindness too soon
for you never know how soon it will be too late
-----Ralph Waldo Emerson

We are Christians and strangers on earth.
Let none of us be frightened; our native land is not in this world.
----- St. Augustine

The professor's project was over. It appeared to have been a success as a result of the students' logic and fact-finding questions. The group -- the "guinea pigs" as Walter claimed -- instead meant a lot to the thesis bound students. They actually admired the professor's wit or luck in finding a gem of experienced human beings. The wiser humans, for their part, felt that the planet would be in good hands in the reigns of these credible young Americans.

Days after, the event story became a routine starting or reference point of conversation, followed by a reminder from Max that a debriefing or some sort of feedback get-together could be arranged. Besides, there was one more person in the team now that, not only played a very robust role in addressing very critical questions from the students, but showed interest in being part of their organization. Karen Summers became that new-found gem. Yet, every conversation pointed to Elvera to take the initiative for such a feedback gathering. Although Elvera agreed with the idea, she also felt that a single purpose debriefing meeting would render their participation as just a business undertaking. She asserted that the preparation for the students' project had been long and fruitful. Likewise, the results had been equally challenging as the narrowed and focused themes impacted their own perspective on life and personal beliefs. Thus, she said that a venue for such gathering should also involve heart and soul elements. In her follow-up e-mail to her friends, her message was succinct and clear. "Listen, brothers and now sister Karen, Max's idea is not only justified but perhaps could be raised to another level. Like joining the useful to the joyful. Let's do such a thing; but let me check with my partner -- the wise man in the house."

∞∞∞∞∞∞

Herbert and Fausto had agreed with Elvera's e-mail message and were certain that something concrete and fun driven would come from either Elvera or the combination of Walter and Elvera. Meanwhile, Herbert and Fausto, by the proximity of their ministries and their growing friendship, would not have to wait for Elvera or for a timeline for any type of discussion on Max's intent. Their telephones – the ever-reliable communication toys – would accelerate the process of learning more. Thus, Fausto called Herbert.

"Good morning Mr. Hawkins. Or dear brother."

"Good morning my friend. 'Mr. Hawkins' has a good ring, for it rhymes with respect. I love 'brother', instead. However, it also implies we are in a monastery. Not yet, brother. I am still married and monasteries do not facilitate co-ed accommodations. What are you up to? Still Sam and the students' thesis?"

"No and yes. No, as far as Sam. And yes, it is about Vera's last e-mail message. You agreed with her suggestion or on her thoughts in delegating part of the solution to Walt. Nothing new here. Max did answer in an identical manner and Karen said she would help Elvera on anything she would need. Therefore, something should happen soon. Still, you and I can talk or find a venue for some useful chatting. It does not have to be always around Sam. Besides, Sam's life is evolving so nicely."

Fausto never took offense by Herbert's more recent references that *The Reformation was over.* He valued Herbert's interjections because they were true and dovetailed with the increased awareness amongst the Catholics and Protestants that Ecumenism was here to stay and should gain more traction. It should get fresher legs and less lip-service. Hence, Fausto meant to elevate Herbert's more ubiquitous reminder to *The Reformation was over* to a mano-on-mano conversation. *"What else is there in Herb's reminder?"* he mumbled to himself.

"Now that Sam is following his improved life's compass you must be lonely. That happens to Catholic priests. But you are

resourceful and can direct your energies towards other challenges."
Fausto did not answer because his DNA did not permit such (idle)
behavior or state of mind. Herbert also thought he had gone too far
with his apparent accusation that Catholic priests, adherents to
celibacy, were lonely. After all, the role of the priests was not
exclusive to following secular undertakings mixed with matters of the
soul. Herbert regretted and said: "first, let me call you brother, too.
Second, sorry for I was out of bounds when I said you were lonely
because you are a Catholic priest. Saints are always challenged; never
idle. You called because you have a question or a concern. Right?"

Fausto just smiled even if Herbert could not see or read it. Then,
laughing, he said: "that was a good heap of manure that could make
Italian kale grow faster. However, your claim is not foreign to me. My
point is that, because we live not far away, we can tackle the students
project before we meet with the rest of the group. I also have a
matter of general interest that can be included in the chat." Herbert
was relieved and, at the same time, now curious about the *other
matter.* Fausto continued, "are you free for some tea at my place? It
is humble but warm. Pick a day at some time in the afternoon of
tomorrow or Wednesday. Can you do that?"

"Yes, I can. I just checked my calendar -- tomorrow or
Wednesday are okay. But, wait. I have a better idea. How about you
coming to my castle for dinner? Like tomorrow night or Wednesday?
Katheryn's treat. She cooks well and we do not fast and abstain from
meat."

"You are on a roll with your zingers. Edmund Conrad would not
recognize you; the strait-laced gent is now a comedian. The answer is
yes -- tomorrow evening. I don't want you to change your mind. And,
I eat anything but pasta, lasagna and pizza. I shall bring red and white

wine. Don't argue with me, now. Just provide the Scotch; good Scotch."

"Well, we are both back in form. See you tomorrow at six. Okay?"

"Okay it will be."

∞∞∞∞

Fausto walked a couple of blocks towards California street, took the street car to Van Ness Ave, took another bus for another mile, and then walked a couple of more blocks to reach Herbert's home. All in less than thirty minutes – including wait time. Although Fausto was very much aware of Californians' love for the car, he was similarly pleased that public transportation was not bad in the city. He rang the door-bell, the door opened and there he saw Herbert in his buttoned-up pullover. Perhaps a common man's cardigan.

They traded smiles and then Herbert, still smiling and hand-gesturing said: "Come on in. On time. Not bad for a man disdaining rules."

"You are still programmed for fun chat. You must have not turned off your computer. Right?"

"You got it." As Fausto entered, Katheryn showed up in her classic apron with a very bright smile.

"Come on in. Oh, well, you are already in. It is an honor to have you in our home. We only connect in official events." Fausto reached for Katheryn's shoulders and delivered the usual light hug greeting.

Fausto followed Herbert to an alcove not far from the kitchen and dining room and waited for Herbert to offer him a drink. Herbert picked up a drink glass, lifted a bottle of Glenlivet and said: "pure shot or on the rocks?"

"On the rocks, please; four or five of those cubes of ice. I know I am committing a sin by adding ice to this great scotch. The authentic Scotch whiskey drinkers would castigate me with their looks." Herbert proceeded to also pour the same scotch for himself, but with less ice – two little cubes.

"Cheers! And to noble friendship." Sticking his head towards the kitchen, Herbert hollered at Katheryn and offered her a drink as well. She said "not yet;" and kept busy.

Herbert made a move towards sitting on the upholstered built-in bench that dressed nicely and conveniently the wall and invited Fausto to do the same. Then, Herbert meant to start the chat while saying that any serious conversation on the students' project could wait for Katheryn's presence, as she had hinted to be added to the exciting professor's project feedback. Fausto showed excitement with the prospects of Katheryn's joining both themes – the students' challenge and Fausto's intriguing swim on the *"Reformation is over."* To Fausto, the latter theme was of far more importance than the students' thesis. To lighten-up the chat or create a pleasant start, Fausto read two trivia questions: "I came across a couple of quotes but do not have the authors' names. Can you tell? The first is like this -- God is preoccupied with everyone; but not to the extent he'll sweep the floors." Herbert liked the quote but could not remember who had said it. Fausto followed with the second trivia quote: "He will not change a date to accommodate your schedule. He'll help you thinking about a reasonable alternative."

"Nope. Can't tell who done it either. But good in enlightening some stubborn or lazy parishioners," concluded Herbert.

∞∞∞∞∞

Dinner was ready and so was the dining room table. Katheryn had it well set – fine but not exquisite cutlery, two plates – one for main course and one for soup – in each individual space. Wine and water glasses ready for the filling, and two candle holders with candles already lit. Perhaps an unnecessary detail as the room was well lit. A little soup terrine was also on the table as well as a small basket with dinner rolls and bread sticks. Once each person occupied their places, Katheryn made a motion to lead in prayer.

"Dear Lord, we are so lucky to have friends to share a meal as much as to share in our mission that you have entrusted to us in life. May we ever deserve your blessings to do good to others." Fausto followed with a well meant "Amen!" Katheryn resumed her hostess' duties: "Although winter is recently over, I still like to make soup. On cold days, especially. It is always convenient and simple to make it." Herbert seconded the idea and added that he would venture sometimes in making soup himself out of left-over main courses. "Help yourselves to the soup," she concluded.

Herbert opened one of the red wine bottles Fausto brought, poured in each glass and proceeded to fill the water glasses, too.

"Thanks, Katheryn, for this very cozy and elegant food entertainment." Katheryn reciprocated with her sincere *it is my pleasure; glad you came* statement. After filling his plate with soup, serving himself of a bread roll and butter, Fausto gave notice of his desire to chat on serious matters. "I am glad Herb revealed your interest in chatting about our extraordinary assistance to the graduate students of philosophy. I am sure our debriefing will not only add value to what we got out of such undertaking but also firm our own beliefs. It was a challenging subject and one where we had to dig for honest answers. I hope the students became more enlightened. However, I think they will be good citizens of our planet."

Katheryn added her own thoughts: "Indeed, I am happy to be able to share in whatever wisdom I have. At least after what Herb dispensed in details. Few, but relevant."

After the meal, which also included dessert of chocolate mousse, Katheryn offered coffee or tea. Although tea was an any-time-any-occasion preferred drink of Fausto, he liked the wine choice; thus, he warmed his glass with a bit more Merlot. After all, he did not have to drive – bus service would still be available -- and while walking the blocks in between bus stops, he would come across some of his friends, some homeless friends. The three, then walked to the living room – a room more family room oriented than the traditional living room. When confronted with help with the dishes, Katheryn insisted that the moment was not propitious for cleaning the dishes, claiming that it would be a task relegated for later to the conclusion of the gathering. "Don't bother. Just leave the plates stacked on the kitchen counter and sink. We'll take care of them much later. I insist. I do."

"So, what did Herb tell you about the project? Something that made sense or inspired you?" started Fausto.

"Not enough. Herb just covered some aspects that drew his curiosity. For instance, he mentioned the early moments when the students, the professor, his assistant and you mingled for a cup of coffee and donuts. Nothing that could be taken as a staged beginning; instead it imparted sincere and warm greetings between strangers with too much at stake. Herb was impressed with the melting the ice."

"Melting the ice. Well put, Katheryn!" replied Fausto.

Herbert added: "Katheryn liked the part where each one of us and the students got name tags. Well, the students already had theirs well displayed. Theirs, displayed their first names – of course, the first only – with some allegoric meaning. For instance, theirs revealed the name followed by a smiling face. And right below, in small but clear print were the words **Yes, we can**. Whereas, ours contained our first names (the only ones disclosed in our profiles) followed by a heart and, on the bottom, the words **So can we**."

"Certainly, this was clever and with psychological meaning. Herb also added, after Mr. Betancourt made a wise remark, that the idea of the names tags as exhibited, was meant to express their belief that your participation would help with their thesis but more so with the idea that their lives to come had to be relevant, filled with cooperation and global meaning." Katheryn paused and then resumed. "To me, this meant that they were serious and credible dialogue participants."

"Good take, Katheryn," said Fausto. "Let me share a useful recommendation." Katheryn frowned and Fausto proceeded, "when you meet Walt don't address him as Mr. Betancourt. He may take an issue with that. Walt is a different animal, the best in any environment, including in the jungle. Just addressing him as Walt would be lovely to him."

Katheryn, after Fausto's recommendation and before he meant to continue, looked at Herbert and asked: "Is he that way, Herb?"

"Yes, he would, dear! He would, even if in a polite manner. The man has manners but his tongue moves faster than his brain. Well, this is the way we have loved to know him."

"I've got to meet this human being."

"You will. If Vera concocts something good you will." Herbert finished.

"Another funny piece was when … Walt," (she hesitated in saying Walt), "was when the dialogues began. Herb said," Katheryn paused and then finished … "go ahead, Herb. Tell Fausto about how Walt was the first to be asked. Tell him."

"Oh, yeah. Fausto also laughed with this one. It was vintage Walt. You see, after the initial introductions and ice-melting exchanges, we were directed to a classroom where two sets of two rectangular tables were displayed side-by-side, face-to-face in a way that there was a pronounced space between the students and us. All six students, with their small laptop computers, sat across from us. They looked like six detectives collecting depositions or the details of a fender-bender chain reaction car accident. Or like we were being interviewed collectively on a murder case. The same question was asked of us but by a different student, in a different manner, tone and purpose. Very clever, very clever. So, it appeared the theme of the question was the same; and yet, it was not."

"So, what is the point?" asked Fausto.

"Don't you remember what Walt said?" interjected Herbert.

"Oh, that moment! Of course, I do. It was funny and it may have set the course of the questions-and-answers game." Finished Fausto.

"Fausto, tell your way; how you recollect it," implored Katheryn.

"Okay, let me see. First, Katheryn, you have to meet this man. Walt is real. I still have Walt's first question memorized. I had to memorize it." Fausto repeated:

So, I am the first guinea pig and you the first Gestapo guy. I like the way you introduced yourselves with warm greetings, fancy and inspiring name tags, as if we were in a Rotarians' annual convention.

All good. But why me? Why the first? Do you plan to dispatch the old man and feel good and warmed up? Let me tell you my dear friend … because you are my friend like my son and daughters are my friends. You had better be real and better have good dirt-smart questions. First, why me? And you – the first of the bad guys?

Fausto proceeded. "I would be scared with that beginning. Anyone would. However, Walt relaxed me and everyone else with his follow-up statement. Here it goes, take a word or two. Isn't that it, Herb?" Herbert waved the palm of his right hand as a sign of agreement and to go-on. Then Fausto continued.

Okay, my friend. Your question has to be about God. Whether he exists or makes sense to smart people that forget knowledge does not come by chance. Whether you think that spiritual books, like the Bible, are products of Voodoo business or not, or you may change the name "God" for another name, it does not matter. It is not that important. Philosophers are called philosophers because somebody thought it would be a cute name, different from a name like someone who fixes your plumbing, heats your home, or anything that makes living somewhat comfortable. Give another name to the Almighty forces that govern our planet, or the universe. Yes, the Bible may look like or sound like a book for children, a book of fairy tales. Or a book about Crime and Punishment; or Christians in the Wonderland. It may be so simple, or somewhat fuzzy and ambiguous. However, tell me – did you want the Bible to narrate stories or be guide books about Bill Gates, Shakespeare, Einstein or Henry Ford? That early in the game? Tell me: is the Bible fake news? Or is it a relevant way for this invisible almighty being to see his creation grow, tweak here and there, break the mold, start all over and then figure out it was not working? Did He not change the mold altogether with the sending of his own son to our planet? The only planet, so far, that has human and animal life like ours. And, the coming of His Son must have been the most relevant change that the Creator could have done. That is love, and more love, and more patience, and love again. And, it is still not working fully. But the only hope in life. Hope that replaces science just for the sake of science.

Fausto concluded: "Everyone in the room was stunned. The professor was less stunned because he had already had a generous dose of Walt. And, the professor adored Walt. He had equally reminded his students that Walt was to be the first; as if to get him out of the way for a good and relevant reason. Walt then changed his tone and posture as if he were the best grandpa one could be, the best to tell stories. The students relaxed, came to earth. Walt, then, finished his now very warm tirade:"

Sorry, my friends for causing you to wet your pants. Sorry! Believe me, I have no interest in scaring the hell out of you. On the contrary, I am proud of all of you for pursuing themes, careers or fulfilling your objectives of wanting to know more. It does not matter how much you have read, how much you really know, nor how much you want to learn. What matters is your seriousness in wanting to know more or the need to follow your heart. I applaud you as much as I have applauded my children, and now grandchildren. It does not also matter if my answers hit the mark. They come from my heart, from my personal narrow world. Go ahead; take me as your grandpa.

"Was that it, Herb? Is that the way you remember? You came close, but not as colorful as Fausto was," added Katheryn.

"Well, not many people can be like Walt or Fausto."

Fausto cracked a mischievous smile and then helped Herbert. "Katheryn, I added my own inflections and words. But I was not too far from what happened."

"Thanks Fausto. And the event went well on both sides of the aisle. In your case, on both sides of the tables. That is what Herb concluded," finished Katheryn.

"Let me tell you, the whole environment was very positive with questions flying and relevant answers making company. I am still thinking about the effects of the whole thing. Do you agree Fausto?"

Fausto liked Herbert's view point. "I do and found some sort of reliable enlightenment. Just being open to relevant or no gimmick questions, caused me to think more; or find a need to pursue some important points the students proposed we research."

∞∞∞∞

"It is getting late and I had another intriguing question. It will be for another time," uttered Fausto. "We must say good-bye."

"Why rush?" stressed Katheryn. "It is only a bit after eight."

"Well, you still have the dishes to do. I could help, too." offered Fausto.

"No way. I have plenty of time and use the occasion to do my mental prayers. Stick around and share your concern," added Katheryn.

Herbert decided to intervene. "Katheryn is right; she is telling the truth. Forget the dishes and tell me what is bothering you. Some more wine?"

"Are you crazy? The cops may ticket me for drunk-walking. But, if you insist, I will fire my question. Burning or not."

"Good," said Herbert. Katheryn showed her approving smile, too.

"Well, my question is beyond a typical or routine question. Otherwise I would ask it at any time. It is a combination of a concern and a strong curiosity. It is based on your more frequent reference to the *Reformation is over* thing. I am not offended in any manner for all of us are always in a reformation mode. Particularly in today's rapid times, changes occur fast and in various degrees and colors. Don't you think so?"

"I agree, Fausto. However, when I mentioned it to you every now and then, I meant to also include myself in the need to reform. You did not get my meaning nor did I expand further on it. But please, share your concern, Fausto."

"Thanks, Herb. Of course, I sensed the remark had to have another purpose. But, like you, I left it at that. I recognize that the Catholic Church, in spite of trying to make amends for our sins of the past, is still dragging its feet towards more collective fruitful dialogue and concrete steps in bridging the gaps. Granted, we have a very ingrained culture and the other branches of Christianity still resent us with some passion. Still, we all are facing some apathy from our followers and finding our numbers dwindling. It is as if we are not relevant in today's world, today's society."

"You are nailing the concern on the head," replied Herbert. Katheryn nodded a yes as well. "But go on, Fausto. By the way, let me excuse myself." Fausto said okay.

Katheryn intervened. "Herb's inference that the Reformation is over also contains a practical point. And we both have talked about the issue. I have followed the Catholic Church in recent times. I have also shared in the bad publicity you have had. You're so global and hear from all time zones. You must get tired of the negatives. However, your positives are equally immense. People, including people like me and Herb, take notice. For instance, your popes have expressed many regrets and apologies for the perceived or real sins you have committed. You have publicly apologized to the Jews for the Inquisition; apologized to the victims of priests' misdeeds, or even for not being more overt against the Nazis and World Wars. People take notice. I am in line with your concern. Herb, applauds Catholic initiatives for being visible in our society. However, we still are too far apart. I suspect that Herb means that your Vatican Council did not produce more robust changes." Katheryn observed Herbert returning and said. "I opened the conversation, mentioned the regrets of the Catholic Church and the need to move faster in steps toward reconciliation."

"That was nice, Katheryn," said Herbert. "Now, Fausto, what do you remember of Vatican II? You were still a kid, right?"

"A lot and not much. I was in High School, but not that versed on the main topics. Remember, Pope John XXIII started the revolution, but because of his death after the Council started taking shape, Pope Paul VI took over. A good pope but not that dynamic and forceful. And the very conservative wing was not too agreeable to the more substantial changes. So, I was not much on par with the big changes. I just remember the more cosmetic changes, like changes in the Mass liturgy and church environment."

Herbert and Katheryn looked puzzled. Fausto continued. "Let me see what I remember then. Today, in the celebration of the Mass, the celebrants face the congregation instead of the old ways of priests turning their backs to us. You see, they used to face the altar. The readings changed from Latin to English. You know, to the vernacular in every country or place. Slowly the singing became warmer and more spontaneous. Right after, we saw the priests' attire, outside the Church, become more contemporary as opposed to the rigidity of the collar, black and cassocks. Lay folks started to get involved in the readings; women did not have to cover their heads or even nuns, in many orders, started relaxing their attire, replacing the long head-to-toe robes for long length skirts and short veils on head coverings." Fausto stopped as Herbert offered an opinion.

"I still remember not long ago when we were in the Vatican, seeing nuns with those long robes and wearing hats looking like bird-wings, and only exposing their faces and eyes. I thought it was cute as opposed to the attires of the other nuns. I also remember hearing that nuns before Vatican II were so austere in schools they ran and other venues." Herbert paused and then said: "Continue Fausto."

"Yes, indeed, funny. Of course, for strange reasons, in the years after the Council, we lost many nuns. One thing that impacted me was the fact it was Pope Paul VI, the first representative of the Church, who addressed the United Nations. The other popes also gained more respect and importance in the world's landscape." Fausto paused again, then told Herbert to hold his opinion for a second. "The liturgy also got much attention in various aspects of the Mass celebration. For instance, the laity started playing bigger roles by doing Mass readings and distributing the Eucharist. I am finished for now; even though I have not addressed my concern about the effects of the Reformation."

"Thanks, Fausto. Besides these cosmetic changes your church undertook, I took notice of the church elevating their role and presence in the world. No other leaders in the various religions were and are taken with admiration like your popes. When they talk, the whole world listens. I value that; not for posture or prestige but for the respect it gets. World leaders take notice when official letters, official proclamations, let me see, you call them Encyclicals. Isn't that it, Fausto?" Fausto nodded and Herbert continued. "These encyclicals call for changes and compel the hierarchy of the church to adhere to or cause the faithful to follow. Actually, it mostly tells the world that is the way the Catholic Church views pressing matters and invites adherence."

"Indeed, these Encyclicals carry power," said Fausto. "So, you're impressed with the Catholic Church's way of doing things, of imposing their dogma."

"I am not talking about dogma, as your dogma sometimes gets you in trouble or extends hurdles and corresponding resistance. In any kind of religion, dogma does some good and some harm. It is inevitable."

"So, in one or two words, you respect and are enamored of the Catholic Church," finished Fausto.

"There is some truth in that. Part of it rests on the fact that when I say, seriously or jokingly, that *The Reformation is over,* it is time for the Catholic Church to pay attention to the many reforms the reformists advocated; and, invite them to your fold, of course, with concrete deeds and overtures. As is, what we get is lip service. I would be comfortable in the Catholic Church environment. I would."

"Meaning that celibacy is in the way. Is that it, Herb? Do you see the same way Herb sees, Katheryn?"

"We are just talking; just pure conversation on a very delicate matter for everyone. And mostly for you, Fausto," replied Katheryn. "I don't see the enormous advantage of creating this obstacle on men that by their talent or vocation could be outstanding leaders of the Church in every capacity. I can't even recall that priests in general were not married in the time of the early Church. I know the gospels where Jesus tells many young men to drop everything, even their families to follow him or gain the Kingdom of God. And, even then and there, Jesus was addressing the young men who had all but meant to use all to buy a place in heaven. Therefore, the Catholic Church, by their stubborn and archaic rules, loses."

"So, let me ask one hypothetical question" Fausto proposed: "If my Church relaxed the rules about celibacy, would you encourage Herbert to trade places? Would he feel at home?"

Katheryn did not volunteer answering the question as she guessed Herbert would. "I already said I would. Yet, not too fast because I am fine where I am. Nevertheless, I would be inclined to make a move if it became appropriate. As it is, there is no hope."

"All good. I value your input because, like you kind of mentioned, I have seen good priests leave the priesthood because they also experienced the desire of being married or having a little family. And, in the early church, some priests were married and others not. The mandate or the rule of celibacy only came many centuries later. All perhaps because of convenience, greater abundance of applicants and also because of economics of the times. In many poor parts of the world, coming to the priesthood brought food to the table and a roof over their heads. I mean their families. Now, Herb, did you always think this way?"

"No, only a few years ago and also since I met you. That is all. Even more recently when I married my niece. Evelyn, that is my niece, you know Edmund's daughter, married a nice young Catholic man. They took their honeymoon only two months after their wedding. Guess where they went and what place they chose for honeymooning?" asked Herbert.

"No idea. To Nepal, for meditation purposes? To the Vatican for a meeting with the Pope?"

"Come on Fausto; I am very serious here. Take a responsible guess!" finished Herbert.

"Sorry, Herb. You are serious and I should respect you for that. But sincerely, other than choosing Bali, I have no idea."

"Okay. Not even me. But Marco, that is my niece's husband, chose to spend more than twenty days on the Camino Santiago. The big Camino! They actually started the Camino in Burgos. My niece told Katheryn they walked over four hundred miles sleeping in hostels and a couple of inns, eating here and there. They claimed the experience rekindled their pursuit of inner peace and life's meaning. I was impressed and moved by their choice."

"Good story, Herb. But anyone can do the Camino. You don't have to be Catholic to take part in the Camino," countered Fausto.

"Correct! I can learn that everyone can do that. However, the point here, is that this is a Catholic tradition. And we can say that there are many other traditions driven from the Catholic faith. Am I getting to my point?" Fausto said yes.

Katheryn intervened. "Here is another one with marginal value; yet, with some credentials to boot. I am giving an example of the universality of the Catholic Church. Pay attention and get the significance. Herb and I take vacations. To Europe mostly. Herb also watches his pennies and values good company. We like to travel in pairs, even though we have attracted larger groups to fit a tourism van of ten to twelve. This trip was to France, Switzerland and the Netherlands. This couple we know well are of mixed religion. He was and is Lutheran and his wife is Catholic. A serious Catholic. We arrived in Paris on a Sunday. It was a matter of price and convenience; stayed at an old but nice hotel in downtown Paris. It was near everything, like Champs Elysée, Louvre and Cathedral of Notre Dame. Alice, our friend, was not happy she had missed Mass -- Sunday Mass. On Monday, that is the following day, we chose to see the Louvre Museum and visit the Cathedral. All went well until Alice reminded us that because she had missed Mass, she planned to make it up on that day -- Monday. So, we joined her more for the gazing of the architectural beauty. It was about ten before eleven, as the custodians or guide in the cathedral posted signs indicating that religious services were in progress – *Silence, respect the religious services*. We guessed it would take some time for the Mass services. Yet, we accompanied Alice. We followed the ritual, understood very little of the language, followed Alice's genuflections or faked what the others did. One hour later, we understood why Alice insisted on attending Mass. At the end, she thanked us and said. 'I am happy, I missed the Sunday Mass but I am certain the Lord accepted the trade-off.' Next, I reminded Alice that she did not know French. She replied: 'I know, but I understand the whole flow of the services. I am thus in solidarity with everyone in my Church and in the whole world.' I was proud of her. I respected more the value of her religion. I still do."

"Thanks, Katheryn. I can see yours and Herb's points."

Herb concluded. "Now, fast forward to the Evelyn's and Marco's wedding. You know it was a dual celebration. Of course, with the exception of my participation in a couple of readings and some aspects of the homily, it was just a Catholic wedding with a Mass like the one we attended in Paris. I felt good and at home in the sequence of the rituals. Very much at home. Can you see my affection for your Church?"

"I do and I do, indeed. And this is the agony I have about the matter of celibacy in our church. And I suppose Pope Francis is getting the heat from both sides. Even within the reality that we must move less timidly towards becoming more relevant to you and other Christian religions. Equally in dealing with the realities that neither have we had net gains in new priests nor is the time ripe for some bold decisions. I fear for the Pope. If the decision, which may take place anytime soon, is for easing up the acceptance of married priests, some imagined bad blood could erupt as well. Or some sort of schism may come again. I fear for many. But for Pope Francis the most."

"I agree. But remember, others would fill the voids," stated Herbert.

"And you would be a candidate, Herb. However, stay where you are. You will be better off staying in the inside than the outside."

"We are just talking. The reformation is actually over and you guys are missing the boat."

"Time to go. It is time to walk and take the bus back home to my hut."

"I can take you back, Fausto. I can."

"Thanks Herb. I will walk and pray and find a soul with whom I can chat. Like old times when I met Sam."

"This was so joyful and productive chat, Fausto," concluded Kathryn.

"Thanks for the meal and great hospitality," finished Fausto.

8

A Sunday barbeque at Elvera's

Sam takes the bait

As we get older, we also get to be wiser.
One watch costing $300 dollars reads the same time as one costing $30.
Being <u>alone</u> in a house of 600 sq. feet is the same as in a house of 3,000 sq. feet.
I hope that one day your (inner) happiness does not depend on material things.
It does not matter if you fly first class or economy.
You'll die if the plane falls and crashes.
I believe that when we have friends, people to talk with, laugh with, sing with, this is happiness.
-----Pope Francis (?)

Two days before the party at Elvera and Walter's was to take place, Elvera received a large business type envelope with the sender's name of the University of the Bay Area. She was happy but not surprised by such receipt. Before opening the envelope, she suspected it could be a certificate of appreciation for their job at the students' thesis project. Instead it contained a handwritten note from Professor Eichelberger and six separate sealed white envelopes with the participants individual names. The handwritten note from the professor was very complimentary of her efforts in keeping the participants motivated in their participation. She then opened her own envelope and read a generic typed letter, but enriched with handwritten personal notes from all the six students. The typed letter was rich in compliments and in promises from all students expressing their commitment to deliver professional and personal value during their lifetime. What charmed Elvera most was the many personal handwritten notes from each student had zeroed in on Elvera's own personality and impact on them. *"How thoughtful and dear!"* she thought. Walter got his own envelope once he arrived home. Both felt rewarded beyond belief.

Elvera recalled with joy that two weeks earlier she had followed Walter's urge to finally stage the thought-over invitation for a barbeque type brunch at their home on an early Sunday afternoon. Spouses of the participants would be invited as well. Herbert had said, and Fausto agreed, they would persuade Sam and Randolph to also come. Fausto even triggered some laughs as he volunteered to pray and cajole Sam to come – two actions in the same motion. Karen Summers had said she and her husband would not miss such an awesome gathering and the possibility of valuable debriefing, as she claimed her previous research expeditions would benefit by the experience gained from the project. Thus, Elvera counted with her fingers how many would join on that late Spring, early Sunday afternoon celebration. If everybody would come, she estimated a number close to a dozen. Herbert and Fausto would take a pass on travelling by BART; instead, Herbert planned to drive with his wife and Fausto, and perhaps Sam, if he finally succumbed to Elvera's bait. Elvera and Walter were excited as a crowd of that size would make the matter far better -- not too many neither too few.

Elvera and Walter were experienced hosts for a rowdy crowd of their large family of two daughters, one son, and their spouses and five grandchildren -- a cozy and self-serve crowd. Small gatherings of two to three couples were the other homogenous crowd, where simple menu discussions found collective agreement. However, a diversified crowd as the one on the agenda, posed some challenges that required better thinking. Not even Walter's golf buddies or other types of food - grilling aficionados would trigger any special treatment. They were at times noisy and happy fellows.

"Vera, cooking for this well mixed but small crowd will be a breeze. Don't know their tastes but couldn't care less. What we have for them could also satisfy the Bishop."

"Bishop? When was the last time you did that? Fed a Bishop? Father Lukas, yes."

"Not at home, but when we helped the Knights of Columbus on a fund-raising party. The Bishop was there. As far as I know, someone claimed the Bishop ate well."

"Why not eat well and enjoy good food? Bishops are human, have bodies begging for nourishment. Did you expect them to fast, to be party-poopers, or show-offs?"

"Honey, don't take me so seriously! That was in jest."

∞∞∞∞∞

Max arrived with his wife, Katheryn; the first to show their faces. Right after were Karen and her husband Arthur Summers. Max was prompt in introducing Katheryn to Karen and then to Arthur. The two couples quickly became no strangers. Arthur said that he was thrilled to come to meet the happy, down-to-earth human being, who could also tell good jokes. Walter took the compliment and proceeded to shake it off with just mild smiles. Instead, he invited Arthur and the arrived guests for some drinks -- whatever was in the ice chests and on the tables.

"Walt, go easy on the drinks. Our guests just arrived and let's take care of other things first," pontificated Elvera.

"Okay!!! As usual, you have the first and the last word," answered Walter. "In this case, fellows, once you are finished with Vera's niceties join me near the grill. Isn't that right?" The friends nodded yes and waited for Vera's house cleaning instructions.

After Elvera staged the house tour, the guests arranged their seating on the patio not too far from the grilling assembly on an "L" shape granite counter. Besides a five-burner grill, a rotisserie skewer completed the grilling toy -- Walter's favorite grilling tool. The counter assembly sported a bar sink on top, a small refrigerator under the counter, space saver cabinets to house a trash can and grilling utensils, and other conveniences. The yard was large, with simple garden architecture whose accents leaned more on efficiency than looks. The grounds were covered either with decorated concrete or clay tiles for orientation and concrete slabs were positioned to lend company to tree and flower pots. The tree pots were of concrete aggregate, but large and deep enough to offer small fruit trees a good habitat. A large and rectangular patio cover was strategically positioned away from the grilling area and almost in line with the family and entertainment room. Under the patio cover, one could see and enjoy the comfort of sectional patio furniture. All were rattan items, consisting of one large lounge sofa, two chairs with ottomans and one coffee table. A portable gas heater was creatively standing at the corner of the sheltered patio. The sets of patio tables and chairs, made of polished wrought iron, spread themselves harmoniously in the various sections of the yard. Anyone with good knowledge of Elvera and Walter's living style could relate the outside living to their personality -- nice, harmonious, clean and efficient. There was no pool that could entertain their children, grandchildren, or even guests. A surprise that when explained, gained the approval of the visitors. The hosts feared safety issues, which they preferred not to manage. A good size and efficient jacuzzi surrounded by Japanese vegetation did the swimming honors instead.

Katheryn chose Vodka with cranberry juice, also a favorite of Elvera. Max took a Corona and Karen joined her husband with glasses of Chardonnay. Walter followed Max's choice. Actually, Walter had almost consumed his Corona. The ice tub was full to the brim.

"Dear friends, we planned for a fun gathering and good food and drink. Vera showed you our modest home and I showed you the way to the fountain of joy. This first serving of drinks is on the house. The others are on your own?! Relax, 'on-your-own' means you will take care of yourselves from this point forward. If your men are the old-fashioned types, they'll take care of their ladies. Vera will take care of herself." He chuckled as the others laughed. "You'll stay thirsty by your own choice. Therefore, don't hesitate to serve yourselves."

"Don't listen to Walt. He always makes this noise. He is a peach and will make your drinks with gladness. However, he has a point -- please feel at home; we have a nice afternoon ahead of us."

A good size tray of avocado slices topped with olives, pickles and roasted red peppers was on display, together with trays of assorted cheeses and smoked salmon. Little slices of roasted sourdough bread brushed with fine olive oil and crackers were tucked in well decorated and Spanish-themed trays. The Betancourt's really knew how to entertain a la middle-class style -- Walter's only class he knew. No upper class or no tailgate entertainment. That was reserved for A's tailgate parties.

The early arrivals -- not really early-birds -- had arrived around the time suggested. The others, for one reason or another, were still at least thirty minutes away. Herbert was not an overly cautious driver. Yet, this part of the Bay Area was not his friendly repetitive destination. Even on a Sunday. Actually, the guests claimed that Castro Valley was in the middle of a safe and easy to find destinations; on the crossroads of three well-travelled highways -- 580 to 80, 880 and a few miles away from 680. Elvera already knew that Randolph would be a no-show. And Sam opted to come by himself via stopping in Oakland in order to check on his missionaries of the street under the stars near the freeway underpasses of downtown Oakland. Actually, Sam's connections and homeless empire extended to the East Bay and some east Contra Costa communities. Elvera, although the hero in cajoling Sam to also show up and rub shoulders with other human beings, thought that her prayers had not been strong enough to nudge the good Lord to perform another miracle on the go.

"Sorry folks. We have some guests dropping off their intentions in having a good time with us."

"Who is not coming or who is coming late?" asked Max.

"We knew by yesterday, that Herbert's wife, ironically also named Katheryn, could not come as they were surprised with last-minute out-of-town guests. Herbert has said that, no matter what, he would come and claimed out-of-town guests were no match for us. We also knew from Fausto that Randolph would not come. That's it. If Sam – the miracle-in-progress – comes, we will ask for the details."

"Really, too bad. For I was dreaming of meeting this modern-day Mother Teresa," said Karen.

"Not only do we feel like an illusion, meeting and chatting with this good man, but Randolph and Sally as well." reiterated Elvera. "I have faith he'll show up. This time he will."

Max added that he barely knew Sam through the three or so events where Sam was cast as the winner of the good Samaritan or "Be-a-Difference-Rainbow" foundation winner. He was real and at the same time an enigmatic fellow. "From what Fausto tells, Sam is letting his guard soften a bit. In fact, we well remember his most recent thank-you speech had far more words and creative messages than his three-worded thank you on the year before."

"Yes, you are right. When I spoke with Fausto at length, confirming who was coming or not, Fausto said that Sam's aging is finally modifying his stance. He claims that Sam has concluded he cannot do it all. Make no mistake; he'll never change his living environment for anything even remotely close to ours. Never! But he also concedes that feeding his buddies with food and protection and, ... and preaching 'get off-drugs,' is a task that is slowly running its course."

"Thanks, Vera," said Arthur. "Sam's world is so distant from ours." Elvera nodded in agreement. "Even Karen tells me what she has learned from you. Can you add more?"

"Of course, I can. Being with him, even for a short time, for he is always looking to escape us, does not trigger tears. But afterwards, reviewing his heroics (he never says it is heroics) he claims with such candor that *if I do this it is because I can … and I did it. It's not a big deal!*" Feeling inner emotion taking hold of her, Elvera stopped, rubbed her eyes with her right hand and proceeded: "*'It is never out of my way. I love sharing the little I possess. For my buddies, it is more than what they have.'* That is a typical phrase of his."

"Wow!!! So, Fausto, the priest, is his guide, his spiritual guide," continued Arthur.

"Fausto fills that role and more. However, both barely entertain long chats. They see each other almost every day; yet, Fausto respects Sam's aloofness. Almost like the aloofness of a businessman. Fausto, a very happy and gregarious servant of the church, thinks the chemistry is in the actions, the mutual trust, and the space in between them."

"So, he depends on Fausto for guidance and material stuff. What else?" inserted Katheryn.

"Let me see what I remember well. Sam needs no guidance, no help or no nothing. Fausto met him years ago, many years ago when Fausto did rounds through the Tenderloin, in downtown San Francisco. He met Sam, exchanged some odd or casual talk; and then they stuck with each other like glue. But this is what glue did — acceptance of each other — with no agreements. Once Sam calculated Fausto was real, he sought the most discrete way to connect with him as needed. Again, actions spoke volumes. Fausto was happy and let his luck roll and roll; until Sam sought Fausto to hold his money from begging. By then, and this perhaps gleaned from Fausto's shrewd covert tactics, Sam gave up drugs. What followed was a natural progress in achieving moderate but measurable success. Money grew to support the buying of food and other stuff the homeless need daily." All were enjoying the little Vera knew and shared. Sensing that, Vera continued. "Sam being clean of drugs, allowed him to apply his own medicine on others. That is, he started a silent crusade to diminish drug trafficking and drug use. Money saved, needed to be kept. Where? Bank accounts? Handling a bank account would be too complicated for Sam, too messy, at least at that junction."

Turning to his wife, Max said: "Fausto acts as the banker."

"How nice. Everybody wins," concluded Katheryn.

"Indeed, Katheryn. This is the typical saga of success begetting success," affirmed Elvera.

"Another question: besides what you said, how does Sam operate?" asked Arthur.

"Nowadays, Sam, with his contacts in our foundation, like Herbert Hawkins, the Lutheran minister, was granted a room in a shelter run by the Lutherans. At first, he refused to use it for his own convenience. Later on, he relented and finds some rest there between his errands in his territory." Elvera paused while the others processed the new emerging good news. "All of these factors, almost unspoken, are breaking Sam's barriers of personal insulation."

"Thus, he promised to join you today and mingle like a brother with us," stated Karen.

"You've got it. It nudged him to respect us the same way we respect his freedom. No guilt feelings. Just the notion that we value him as much as his friends value him. There is no interference on his mission, if it is a mission. I told him: we all can be of value to one another. Or like employees, at times, influence bosses."

"You said that? Like a motivation moment?" retorted Arthur.

"Just like that." Now turning to Max: "you don't mind me saying this; but I chose an appropriate moment of solitude and asked God to intervene, not for pride but to expand His reach." She held her tears. "And, He delivered. Unless we get a call from Sam saying he had to help someone in need. But I did my part; the rest belongs to God."

All got up and walked around the yard. Walter thought that Herbert and Fausto would be arriving soon. Indeed, the doorbell rang at the door, bringing their attention towards the house.

"Halleluiah. You arrived, and no Sam!" blurted Elvera.

"No Sam, but he will come. He said he will. He called me from the train and needed someone to pick him up. I do not know the station and we did not want to come late. Thus, when he arrives someone needs to get him," stated Fausto.

"I will do that." said Arthur. "I want to benefit from the miracle." Upon being asked about the station, Arthur said: "I know the station quite well. Just ensure he knows what I look like."

∞∞∞∞∞

Fausto and Herbert greeted the other guests. Herbert said: "It is good to have female guests in this gathering -- like you -- Karen and Katheryn. I feel bad my wife could not come."

Katheryn retorted: "I hope Max keeps me in the loop. I heard so much about you folks that benefits my transition into the retirement age." Max, Fausto, Herbert and Arthur gave notice they still worked for a living. Karen dismissed her almost faux pas.

"Welcome; welcome." said Elvera. Then added, "Walt, we can do this again; can't we? Like having another barbeque party soon?"

"We can do this again or give them the keys to the house -- like an Airbnb thing. Without fees!" Those who heard Walter's joke felt it was too intellectually funny -- thus laughing their lungs and hearts out.

"What happened?" asked Herbert. "I did not hear the joke."

"Never mind, Herb. That was another one from Walt," finished Max.

∞∞∞∞

"Where can I help? I know Arthur... that is you name ... right?" Arthur nodded yes and Herbert continued. "Arthur is picking up Sam. Sam knows what you look like. Don't ask questions. Act normal."

"What's the fuss? We both are human beings. Right?"

Herbert replied with no hesitation. "I apologize for the quick advice. But there is a reason for me saying that. We all tend to be kind and useful. Patronization comes along with our manners." All were still puzzled. "If he talks, talk too; if he does not say a word, say nothing. Once he gets here, we ambush him. Get it?"

"The way you put it or place him, it is quite like talking with a nerd from Mars. I will do my part. Don't worry fellows; I will pretend not to ruin the party."

"Sorry, Arthur if I hurt your feelings. It was not meant to. However, it is proper that someone like you -- he does not know -- picks him up. Sorry again!"

"Don't worry. I understand or understood in a few exchanges that in spite of this man's great deeds there is a caveat. I will remember it, for I want to meet this man up close."

Arthur departed for a twenty-minute round trip to the Bart station in Castro Valley. The others joined Walter and shared in his good assortment of liquor; though the men preferred wine and beer and his great zingers. Walter was in great spirits because he felt at home with this new set of friends and acquaintances. *Change is good for you*, he mumbled to himself.

"Let me see … Sam is converted and Randolph is gone or will be gone." Said Walter. "You are a miracle Father Mancini. It was due to happen. It was due."

"Walt, if my memory serves me well, I am going to use an analogy -- the gospel you used with the professor. Do you remember that scene when you reprimanded the professor?"

"No, I do not remember it. I had to be drunk then…"

"I know you remember; you're just pulling my leg. The point here is that we never do or achieve something big alone. Others, named or invisible, play roles in the transformation of something big, something impactful. Everyone plays a role. However, Sam played a role on his own, still to be proven transformation. This must have been achieved based on the experiences with himself as much as with us. Granted, we did provide help with altruistic purposes and honorable ideas."

Fausto continued. "You called me Father Mancini, didn't you?" Walter said he did. "What was the deal?"

"Because I respect you a lot beyond being friends. That is all."

"Okay, Mr. Betancourt, I respect and admire you as well. Calling me Fausto sounds a lot better."

"You're right. We are even."

"Good idea. Now to Sam … let's have him feel the comfort of something that he was far from being a part of. Let him find his place in this gathering. I plan to have a good time and Walt is a good cook and Vera is tops on the list. Let's celebrate some good things in life. What do you say Max? You brought your wife, too. What a treat. What a gift, Katheryn!"

Katheryn smiled but stayed motionless. Max displayed just pure pride.

Father Mancini continued and directed his comments to all. "I am going to have a drink. You, Herb, just drink wine and not much more. You'll do the driving and need to stay sober. We cannot afford to have the police fine two members of the church, including an emissary of Mother Teresa." He paused and then said: "Thanks, Vera for staging this thing."

"It was not my idea. It was Walt's."

"Then let's drink to Walt. Everyone, lift your glasses!"

"Did you drink anything before we came, Fausto? Too much wine in church? If it is, no more booze for you." exclaimed Pastor Hawkins.

"I guess we are in a great mood for chatting and drinking. Walt already preached the command that we have to help ourselves to drinking. He did the first serving. Now, can you tell us something about Randolph? His going away from Sam and San Francisco?" asked Max.

"I can, but I prefer Sam to tell it. It may help his motivation to share. It is a good theme and a necessary answer. Can we do that? Wait for him?" All agree they could and would.

∞∞∞∞∞

"What do you consider a good theme in the Catholic Church?" asked Arthur.

"Nothing about the sins of my Church! March-Madness is over, University of Virginia won, the Giants continue to flounder in their home opener, the Warriors are hot. I know, I know Walt loves his A's. Anything A's and Raiders!"

"Well, if one is serious about religion, the Catholic Church exists because there are sins and sinners. The way I read the gospels that Jesus preached, He came to the world because of the sinners; the others were already on their way to heaven. Don't you agree? They had purchased their tickets. Right?" Max, the agnostic who had read more books about religions, talked with authority and not sarcasm, they surmised.

Fausto intervened; he had to, for he had started the hinted themes. "For those that do not know Max, may find his statement ironic or wrapped in sarcasm. For you, Karen and Arthur, Max has read more material on religion than Herb and I have done in preparation to become religious servants. He did that for different reasons; yet he did it. Now, about the Catholic Church and its sins, it is a fact that makes me pause and dig for valid answers. And since we had that meeting with students of Theology, Philosophy, etc. last month talking about the Catholic Church is no mystery. Yes, we have sinned in many ways -- in the past, not distant past and in the present. It keeps us humble, at least it should."

It was a lengthy confession that others felt free to talk about. Katheryn took the first step. "Fausto, I know about you, logically from Max. Likewise he admires you for being authentic. I am not a professed Agnostic but respect my husband and follow him. However, I can think and make decisions by and for myself. For instance, I know enough about the Catholic Church. Particularly since your Pope John … yes, the XXIII, the nice round face chubby Pope, your church has become more open, more gregarious. You made tons of progress towards conciliations not only to other religions but to the world itself. You have and continue to permeate in the life of society --

modern and old society -- by your hands in many facets of life. At every turn we read about Catholics here, and Catholics there. You deliver a tremendous amount of religious vibrancy in many things you do."

Katheryn stopped and then asked if she was extending herself so much, like invading dangerous territory. She got the message that her inspired words should be said. "Good, thanks. However, the ugly moment or stage you are suffering from is also of your own. I mean the sex scandals caused by bad priests, human beings that commit sins, the way you describe grave errors. We all make mistakes. Everybody does. So, the church through transactions in matters of the spirit, of some sort of divinity, are also run by humans. And we know what humans are and do at times. In part your faithful think that by dressing in special clothes and displaying special collars, you would become saints on the go. That is the problem that the faithful mismanage -- expectations from you and none from them."

"You are so correct, Katheryn," replied Fausto. "This in part should be told to our parishioners. Many have this illusion that we are or are supposed to be saints -- all the time. The other thing I agree is that we should be accountable and held to a higher level, higher standards. No tip toeing around... and should get out when we mismanage our mission."

"I agree," added Herbert. "We should be held to higher examples."

"Now that you allowed me to go on, let me add a few ironic remarks," asserted Katheryn. "Pedophilia is bad because it deals with minors, mostly innocent and green young people. It is violating their innocence, their trust. However, it happens in all sectors of society. I suppose in more segments of society than in the Catholic Church, particularly in schools, particularly in the schools' sports activities; as well as within families. You name it. But listen to me on this point. I am going to make a comparison with a large banking institution I worked for twenty plus years. Yes, the big Bank of America. The comparison is back in the late seventies and early eighties."

She caught her breath and looked at the listeners with keen attention. They had reciprocated with obvious curiosity. "During that period, banks -- all banks -- were consolidating operations at a fast pace. Like closing branch units, buying smaller banks or merging with larger institutions. Bank of America, being the biggest then, was in the middle of this fever; yet, they moved very slowly. Wells Fargo Bank, BofA's nemesis, took no prisoners, and led on the changes. And, by that, they became the darling of Wall Street. Are you seeing where I am going? Like comparing Bank of America, an original and vibrant institution, ubiquitous to the core, with the Catholic Church? Both huge and with enormous presence; yet slumbering along."

"Here is the comparison: At that time, Wells Fargo Bank identified what areas, what branches to consolidate or close. In two years, they had their plan executed to perfection. They received a lot of bad press and moved on. BofA, instead must have done the same research and developed an action plan. However, they did in installments, like during eight to ten years, and got bad press for that long. Can you see the agony and the time wasted? Wells Fargo did it quickly and zipped through the market place with very few scars. BofA? Well, you get the picture."

"The way I match your comparisons is that the Catholic Church should have handled the problem with pedophilia like Wells Fargo Bank with branch closures! Quickly and with determination," interjected Pastor Hawkins.

"Exactly! The Catholic Church, throughout the world, because they are so global, should have recognized that too much smoke had to have come from real fires." Katheryn paused, and turning to Father Mancini, asked: "when did this thing of pedophilia in the church start?" Fausto said it was at the turn of the century. "Here we go; we are talking about over a dozen years. And now the other parts of the world are surfacing with the bad news. By the time this finishes, it is like an eternity. It is like the priests' scandals are on-going events."

"I told you Fausto," said Herbert. "The reformation is over, over four-hundred years old. Now, your church is taking another beating; instead they should, as Katheryn said, have addressed the problem right away, admitted they made mistakes, dealt with it, made reparations, fixed and got it over with. I have come to admire the Catholic Church -- so universal and relevant."

"Thanks Herb. I know and I pain from the matter. Still the Church is lucky, very lucky. Although there have been some exaggerations, there are many cases or examples that have not come to the surface. Many of the abused never filed charges. They most likely suffered, dealt with the pain, and then moved on with their lives. I fear more for the number that did not come out with their sufferings and legitimate complaints. Well, God will help. But we must do better."

"Thanks, Katheryn, for such dramatic but very useful enlightenment," concluded Elvera. "Okay, let's choose another subject. Walt is right, we must refresh our glasses and enjoy the appetizers."

"It was my pleasure! I have admiration for the Catholic Church."

Noise came from the side yard gate. Arthur and Sam had shown up -- happy.

∞∞∞∞∞

"Welcome dear Sam. You look good. And thanks for joining us."

Sam did look good -- a far cry from homeless attire. Nothing upscale -- whether casual or outdoor party dressing. His pants were of a faded and worn corduroy grey, matched by a black "V-neck" sweater, also faded with grey sneakers. He brought no cap to cover his head, still showing healthy dark and sandy hair now cut almost crew cut style; with subtle voids on the side. Perhaps someone of his homeless nation must have cut it at a YMCA bathroom. His beard was noticeably two weeks old, equally revealing shades of grey. He had turned sixty-two; thus, his posture was indicative of any man that age. He looked somewhat less old than when doing his thing at his environment. He was presentable; meaning he respected his invitation as one good guest would.

Sam directed himself towards Walter. Both, spontaneously, greeted each other with their right-hand knuckles and laughed. A greeting the other guests took notice. Sam then glanced at the other guests spread around the terrace. Elvera, seeing the guests almost begging for a good transition to introductions, said: "Okay you all know Sam or heard of him. Let's introduce ourselves to him so that he can feel at home. Can we do that?" Everyone nodded with relief. "So, let's start with the folks guarding the grill and booze in the bar area." All beckoned with gusto, including Sam.

"Well, I started and I introduced myself to Sam already as I picked him up at the station. By the way, Herb, good description of me. Sam had no fears jumping in the car. He guessed he was not being kidnapped." Herbert offered a contrite smile. "One more time, my name is Arthur Summers." Elvera waved Arthur to complete the introduction. "Am I supposed to say what I do for a living?"

Elvera telegraphed a sure yes. "I am an attorney by trade; family law and preparing myself for the transition to the good life of retirement within a few more years."

Elvera was all smiles with Arthur's long introduction. "Thanks Arthur!"

Next, and near the grill, was Father Mancini. Fausto waived his right hand and said "Hi!"

Next, the grill master followed suit with his held right hand and said "Hi, here."

Elvera, following the circle, just smiled and passed her turn to Herbert, who prompted the same greeting as Fausto. Karen was effusive with her smile at Sam and said: "My name is Karen Summers; married to that gentleman over there, preparing himself to invade my territory. Don't you think so? Like Vera and Walt? Both semi-retired are invading each other's space -- time and real space." Elvera dismissed Karen's truth and hinted for her to tell what she did. "Okay; I am a free-lance writer, get paid to do what I do and perhaps I will write about the professor's project and this gathering today. No, I do not take pictures. I will, but will not share them at all."

"You better not; unless we consent," said Max.

After the laughing and the teasing came Katheryn's turn. "My name is Katheryn and married to this lovely man; yes, on my right. I was in the retail banking business for over twenty years and now I am a permanent consultant to a laborers' retirement fund; that is, making sure their savings are responsibly managed and invested."

"Hi, I am Max and like all of us, proud to know Sam. He is someone to be proud of; it is an honor being around him." Tears were about to run from all guests' eyes. Sam just looked down towards the ground.

"Very good, very good. Now that we know each other, let's make the train run. Walt will explain how we stage the grilling. Some of you already savored his grilled sausages. Help yourselves with more of the other appetizers and drinks, too. Remember, help yourselves." Turning to Sam she asked him what he wanted to drink. Sam chose coke and fetched one from the ice bucket near Walter. "Now, Sam, join me in the kitchen. Okay, Sam?" Sam did not wait a second; he promptly followed Elvera.

Walter explained how the barbecue would evolve. "I have here four glass trays with the items to be grilled. You see ... the typical vegetables for grilling, which includes cut pineapple, a tray with small cuts of chicken breasts and thighs, another one with seafood, like scallops and tiger prawns, and another with cuts of pork loin. I have here two bowls of liquid dressing and two canisters of dry herbs; also, garlic salt and pepper if desired. Got it?"

"I do not get it, Walt," said Max.

"Okay, Max, you are new to my grilling, and I will explain." The others were relieved that a genuine explanation would surface. "Other than grilling hamburgers and hot dogs, all of us have different taste buds. All of you can create your grilling items by using these skewers --- bamboo skewers." The teacher was getting the students' attention. "You will prepare your own or tell me what you wish. Or I may grill, individually, all items and then you will choose what you want, afterwards."

"For instance," said Herbert, "I can choose a skewer with the fish and the vegetables or wait for you to grill all separately and then we can serve ourselves?"

"I guess we are getting there. Anyone with the same idea?" said Walter.

"In this case I will choose what Herb chose but with chicken instead. Can you make my skewer with chicken and vegetables?" voiced Katheryn. Walter said it was fine and doable.

The others, including Max, Fausto, Arthur and Karen instructed Walter to grill the items separately and then avail themselves of the good stuff as they pleased, possibly a piece of each. Walter said that was a good choice.

Meanwhile Elvera was explaining to Sam what she had to accompany the grilled items. "I've baked lima beans with celery, mushrooms and thinly cut carrots. I added some cubed tomatoes just to give color. I also have in the oven …" Elvera opened the large gas oven "… ten ears of corn on the cob, you can see, nicely wrapped in foil paper, which I previously rubbed with a little salt, pepper and butter." Sam was happy for he guessed that Elvera would give him chores.

"Can I help you in any way, Mrs. Betancourt?"

Elvera thought that the progress she had achieved with Sam should be extended to other areas. "Sam, look at me. If you call me Mrs. Betancourt, I will call you Mr. Williams. Can you see?" Sam said he comprehended. "Call me Vera and I will call you Sam. Is this a deal?" Sam reluctantly agreed, stating it would be difficult for his habits had been ingrained for years. Elvera said: "Just try, Sam. Just try. Okay?"

"Mrs…., I am sorry, V…era, it will take time for me to get used to calling you by your first name." Regrouping himself he said "this is a very nice and big house. Your family must come here often."

"Sam this is a good house, built on more than one-acre lot. We purchased it thirty years ago and had practically no neighbors. Now we have nothing but new developments. Walt added almost two thousand square feet, up and around, added an adjacent two car garage and a small workshop. He likes to entertain himself with his hands. You know, besides playing golf." Sam was excited with the warm and logical explanations coming from Elvera.

"The outside is large, nicely decorated and built. I am happy for you. You are a very nice lady."

"Thanks Sam. Beyond the patio and fun area, we have about a half-acre in the back separated by a latticed fence, which is also separated by shrubbery. There, Walt grows his vegetables. He loves to grow his own legumes. He spends hours and hours. There is a garden tool shed nicely surrounded by fruit trees."

"Thank you, Vera for the explanation. I also remember my grandpa's little plot in Southern Georgia. I loved hoeing with him." Tears came to Sam's eyes. Elvera turned away for he remembered his grandpa and said little about his mother and father or the rest of his family.

"Sam, you can join the guests. I will ask you to help me when the rest is ready. Okay?"

"I prefer to see the vegetable garden. Can I do that instead? Call me when you need me. Okay?" Elvera was happy Sam was finding bridges to his past. She thanked the Lord.

∞ ∞ ∞ ∞

The guests were already finding their niches -- spread around two patio dining tables and/or keeping company to Walter who dazzled them with stories about his A's and Raiders. They knew his golf scores were high, although he took the accolades in stride.

Elvera came from the kitchen with a large white business type envelope. All looked at her and at the envelope she was waving.

"Folks, please pay attention to something very important I have for you. This envelope, from professor Eichelberger, arrived here last Friday afternoon. It was addressed to me and, when I opened it, I found individual envelopes for each one of us that participated in the students' thesis project."

"Wow! How nice. What else?" asked Karen.

"Oh, a letter from the professor saying I was so good and smart by influencing you all to be good Samaritans. Am I not smart? Like Walt?" Walter laughed almost to the point of choking. She continued. "Just a thank you from him. Why don't you open your own envelopes, read the message and decide if we should have some kind of debriefing?"

Elvera distributed all of the envelopes. All appeared very concentrated in the reading – one time, a second time and then lifted their heads towards Elvera. She then said: "So, what do you think? Any reason to say anything? Or drink and debrief?"

Karen broke the silence. "I like what these young people did. Very classy. However, I see no value in any kind of debriefing. It appears that what happened was good; the students valued our input and now they show credible gratitude. I'd rather learn more about ourselves and validate Walt's great cooking. Well, it is just my opinion."

Max kind of seconded the motion as if it was a motion on a real meeting and waived his glass of wine. The others nodded agreement with a thumbs-up approval -- a definite sign that, the motion by Karen, passed.

Fausto added. "How about you Mr. Chef Walt? Anything different?"

Walter thought over and then said. "Vera gave me the letter when I came home last Friday. I read it, thought about the various handwritten messages on that kind of official stationery and I felt good, emotionally good. First class! The guy who asked me the first question was very thoughtful. I like that young man." Walt stopped, wiped his cheeks with the edge of his hand and stayed unusually pensive. The others dared not to question him further.

Elvera intervened. She went to the kitchen and returned with Walter's letter. "Well, that young man that Walt almost scared the pants out of, wrote an emotional message." She proceeded in reading it: "'I would love to adopt you as my grandfather. I never knew my maternal grandfather and the paternal one was not that kind to me. Thus, I learned nothing from either. You could inspire me in life. You are so lovely raw and credible. The world is better because of folks like you. Thanks grandpa.'"

"Let me start my grilling. My debriefing is done," said Walter.

"Certainly, we are done. We all behaved as '*Be a difference rainbow'* members," concluded Max.

"Thanks, people. Let's resume the fun." Said Elvera.

They all walked towards their chosen spots and proceeded to restart the fun.

"Max, I learned that your grandfather was an Atheist and activist in labor causes," started Karen politely in her desire to know and create solid intellectual talk. She also felt that Max was a good un-parochial dialoguer, as her friend Elvera had hinted one time.

"Yes, yes and no. Let me explain. He was not an open activist but supporter and representative of laborers' causes. He fought for workers causes, for labor relations justice. As an Atheist, from the first time I understood these labels -- religious, Atheist, oblivious to religion, not caring about anything socialism, or just anything, I followed him as an obedient but silent atheist. I guess I followed with my heart. I remember him always bragging about the value of Atheism, in relation to capitalism versus communism. By then I would come to understand that there were two sides."

"Sorry for invading territory that is more a private than open field. However, if you don't mind, can you elaborate?" Karen asked.

"Not at all." Max offered a mild smile, was happy to entertain conversation on a matter dear to him; and in this case, it was with an interlocutor that was credentialed in exploring human life and substantive human stories. In fact, he liked her on the first day they were together on that joint project -- the professor and his students research for exam thesis. "I love and always find satisfaction in clearing up what I view being and existing some misconceptions. My grandfather loved me a lot and thought I would be a follower of his doctrine." Karen smiled happily. "However, observing and enjoying my father and my mother's neutral views and my Uncle Fredrick's way of living, I decided to love him back, but not to espouse his culture. For instance, he was a fan of Karl Marx, but not necessarily of communism as a whole. He felt communists were brutal and meant to exercise excessive power over the masses as much as capitalism exercised economic power by deception. So, fighting for workers' rights only occurred on neutral ground."

By then, Fausto and Herbert had joined the conversation. Walter was happy with his beer and seeing the master pieces of his grilling coming to fruition.

"Can you break this in segments?" asked Herbert.

"Yes, I can. Whether you are an Atheist or neutral in anything like religion, what matters for real people who care about their rights, is to fight for these. However, capitalism has a way of misguiding or misleading people. It finds obstacles, creates economic disparities and then teases people with table crumbs. In Reagan's time, it was taken as "trickle-down" economics or politics. The rich get richer as long as there are some food leftovers for the workers, for the bottom line of society. Can you see the point? Certainly, I am exaggerating the reality for there are many, many people in business that do the right thing. And these are never targeted by activism. Justice must be made here. Nevertheless, let me tell you ..." Max stopped to rearrange his thesis ... "for those of you who remember economics in school must recall Adam Smith's theory on capitalism." Most gave an affirmative nod. "If Adam Smith would return from the grave, he would be appalled by the deceit of the economic and financial powerhouses at the moment. His doctrine of free capital was meant to involve everyone and not the elite -- the manipulators of value and money. Smith felt if capitalism or free markets were done right, all classes would benefit, and the tide would rise for all -- for all." Max stopped and then said: "I want to answer Karen's question about my grandfather and not about politics. Otherwise, she is going to think I am an agitator. I have enough labels that I want socialism in America. As if socialism is an evil term. Americans love labels."

"Go ahead Max. We know you well, and we admire you. You are a noble American. Answer Karen's concern," interjected Fausto.

"Thanks, Fausto. About my grandfather, the question was that his pet peeve was about religion, the existence of God, etc. I have the same issue as he had. I respect religions for they have like everybody else an investment in people's rights and people's well-being." Max paused, then inferred that his uncle Frederick could handle a good quarrel about the matter. Then stated, "he had the same DNA as my grandfather but with opposing views on society, different ways of living. My father, by temperament was docile. End of the talk! I loved my grandfather as much as he loved me. Still, as I grew to see the world with a different pair of eyes, I politely disavowed my allegiance to his view. He was a good man. That is all I can say."

"I suspect you want to put an end to this conversation. But the thing of religion which you did not agree with him intrigues me. How did he display his displeasure? Why beat on religion?"

"I understand your question; we could spend the whole afternoon and night on this matter for I was close to him and heard his little sermons on the matter. For instance, and as it relates to the exploitation of human beings, especially, or the working-class in particular; adding value to the acquisition of wealth, I recall phrases like these: religion is a spiritual booze that causes submission; capitalism exploits human beings; or that humans are enslaved by capitalism and then take shelter in religion! In my book this is philosophy. But he was not altogether correct. Because I read of popes, in their encyclicals, lash out at these capitalistic pronouncements. I read them."

"Indeed, it is philosophy at its best. Unfortunately, the world moves on and the majority of people live on morsels from the tables." said Karen; then concluded, "Max you're so fair on your views. Thanks."

Max gave no clue he would add more to Karen's apparent conclusion. Karen recharged her beliefs -- "no wonder you folks are such enlightened people. I mean all of you. Look at your differences and how well you respect each other and each other's view. Amazing! I'd better start drinking out of your fountain of love, respect and intellectual cohesiveness ... Where are you, Vera?" Vera did not answer, she was out of their reach. "Certainly, I will insist that you include me in these matters involving such magnanimous people," concluded Karen.

"I agree with Karen. The more I learn about you -- from your friends -- the more I find myself on your team. Get me in, too," finished Katheryn.

"The meal is ready," said Elvera, who just showed up after consulting with Walter. "You can see we have two dining tables -- one large that can accommodate six and another -- that round one -- can accommodate four or more. By the grill area counter -- opposite the grill, we can seat four more. However, since we are not a big crowd, perhaps we can occupy the two tables."

Walter washed his hands in the sink, wiped them (under the disapproving look of Elvera) on his apron. Walter nicely waved her off. Then said: "Where is Sam?"

"In your meditation grounds -- your vegetable garden. I'll get him."

"You also have a vegetable garden, Vera?" asked Max.

"I do and I also enjoy it. Walt does all the work -- yard and the vegetable garden. I love my roses and flowers, and pick up the fruit from the trees." She stopped then resumed by saying *I forgot something; what was it?* Ah, it was about Walt's meditation refuge. I can vouch for him. While there, I would occasionally see him talking to himself. And, during summertime ... a couple coronas helped."

"It beats talking to her!" replied Walter. Elvera held her rebuttal back, preferring to gesture something else.

Max laughed and said: "So, you have a plot of land that grows vegetables. That is nice. Is the garden big?"

"Big enough to produce some vegetables year-round. It is almost two thirds of an acre. Go and see after we finish eating."

After Sam retreated from the meditation grounds, and guests chose their places, Elvera hinted for a prayer moment. "Shall we? Not a real prayer but a way to validate this nice gathering."

"Vera, if you're thinking about us, we love prayers; they do good. Max may have already given you our view on this thing. We are living creatures -- prayers are logical."

"Thanks, Katheryn. I suggest that our servant Fausto does the honors. Okay Fausto?" asked Elvera.

"Let's gather and stand in a circle; hold hands and close our eyes. Think about this gathering, about what it has meant to you, about what the gifts of each other mean to each one of us, for we are pure gifts from heaven; think about how you can influence others to choose peace and love instead of rivalry and hate, of how you can be even more significant to others; how you can make a difference as in "Be-a-Difference-Rainbow." They followed Fausto's instructions, joined hands and stayed motionless for two minutes. Then Fausto said: "Creator of the world we live and know, send your spirit of creation to us in a more clear and obvious way, so as to validate that we were made in your image. We love what you did; help us to convince others to care more, love and give of themselves more."

"Thank you, Father Mancini," said Karen.

"You have a real way with words -- words that convince," added Katheryn.

Clapping her hands, Elvera concluded: "Let's eat and talk and be merry!"

The three ladies and Sam sat together at the table of four (or five if they dared to squeeze some space). Sam was happy he was sitting with Elvera. The others had the large patio dining table to themselves.

∞∞∞∞∞

"Now I believe that your golf score is real. Your cooking or your grilling is superb. Invite me again," said Arthur with convincing joy.

"Can you invite us again?" asked Max. "I had heard before that you were a master at grilling…" Walter did not let Max finish.

"And you did not believe me?!" asked Walter. "Shame, Mr. Bingham!"

"Okay, I should be reprimanded. Try again and I will ask for a 'Michelin' rating. Deal?"

"Max, rating or no rating, you are welcome anytime. Even if you never convert!" exclaimed Walter.

"To what? A good grill-man? Actually, you can grill both ways: on the grill and now you are grilling me. You will succeed when you buy the best bottle of Rioja!" replied Max.

"This is a good start --- a duet of smarts!" entered Herbert on the game of words. "It sounds like Spanish wine, this thing of Rioja. Is that it, Walt?"

"I like Rioja wine. However, being Basque is one thing; being from French Basque is another."

"No kidding, Walt. Two different things!?"

"Yes, my dear Herbert. Still, all wine is good. California leads the way. Let's enjoy the meal as there is lots of food, and the afternoon is so young. I even bet we have ample room to nap or sleep if some of you do not pass the sobriety test." Finished Walter.

"Good idea; can we talk about Sam and Randolph? It is so precious that Sam is here with us. He got attached to Vera," said Arthur.

"This is a miracle, Art!" said Herbert. "Don't you think so, Fausto?"

"I do. Perhaps this is a turning point for Sam. Could this be tied up to Randolph? Could this be a message for him to also take a look at himself? Could this be a message from God that he cannot carry the world or the world's misery by himself. Or, is it the smarts of these many years of helping others, and teaching others to help others and themselves finally banging at his own door? Or, is the good he does boomeranging on him?" Fausto paused, looked at his interlocutors, and finding nothing but awe, continued ... "It sounds like that I am preaching or found my way to let what I am enjoying this afternoon spill over now. Thanks Walt. Pulling your leg, saying funny things at your grilling talent is one thing. But I will repeat this one thing – the barbeque is awesome," stated Fausto with pleasure.

"Believe me, I was not nervous you guys were coming. I love doing barbeques, and everyone who can do some cooking will not screw up the grilling. I am pleased you are enjoying yourselves. As for me, I am happy listening to your moments of inspiration. Better than some Sunday sermons I hear at times." Father Mancini smiled and looked at the others for consensus. Walter finished his monologue. "Sorry, Fausto. Priests or homilists cannot be at their best all the time. Anyway, tell us some more about Sam."

Max asked a question instead: "Then, Randolph is gone and this may be affecting Sam?!"

"Yes, I think this and perhaps many other events are impacting Sam. Randolph has not gone away yet. He was supposed to go this past week. However, there were other things that delayed them. I even went with Randolph and Randolph's girlfriend to Saint Vincent de Paul in San Francisco to buy things for them, courtesy of the Conference's generous voucher. We bought some additional clothes and two small carry-on bags. The buying caused Sally to get a larger piece of luggage, too. Both are leaving this Tuesday via the old Greyhound bus way. Do you remember the old commercial -- *Go Greyhound and leave the driving to us.!?*" They did remember.

The others smiled broadly and Fausto continued. "Sam is over sixty; he has been doing this business of homelessness and helping homeless folks for over two decades; I think before I even came to San Francisco. Like in any of us, things get old, things get to you, you get frustrated like Mother Teresa may have found moments of stress, of no ending poverty, and then something else, like God saying you need help, you need rest and ... boom! It strikes on your head. I pray that all of this is causing him to process changes in him and his environment. Now, Vera the link. She is a woman ... and bang ... he softens up. Take a look without looking. Can you see how comfortable he is with them? Vera, the link!"

"I don't have my own take, because this is the first time that I am involved with you folks. It sounds like a lot has gone in this man's life and life itself is finding him now. The cycles, I guess." Arthur intervened and the others nodded. "So, the way I've quickly learned is that Randolph helped Sam in helping the other homeless. And, Randolph by moving away is causing changes -- emotional and behavior changes -- in Sam. Can these be life or direction changes in Sam? Can he survive or, like Randolph, cause him to find another venue, another route in his life?"

Herbert tried to answer but then deferred to Fausto. "Well, before I mention Herb's influence in Sam, let me add something that I believe through experience. Just as in real life, when genuine good Samaritans do favors to people, it is like they innocently or in innocuous ways also own a piece of those helped. Sam, by being around us so often, naturally surrenders to realities, softens his way of being active, slowly reveals his ever-concealed emotions. Herb has come to know Sam by virtue of his church sponsoring a shelter; and also, by learning more first hand. Sam acknowledges this; Sam kind of finds that we two, in our own responsibilities as clergymen, are real --

we love what we do. He is finding that loving what he does also has shortcomings, barriers, bad days. It is life being what it is. I don't mind going to the streets to help Sam solve a case. For instance, Herbert helps him in other ways. When they meet at the shelter, he sees Herb naturally adding value."

The others looked at Herbert. While Fausto hesitated, Herbert continued deferring the narrative to him. "What I guess I am seeing now, is that things change, even if the needs for his help do not. He is using his smarts to accomplish perhaps the same things as before. But street needs keep growing, like never ending. Then, his experiences, he tells me, reveal that not all homeless people are the same, not all have the same needs, or agree to be helped in a logical way. Remember, the homeless world is similar to your and my world -- give or take an inch. It is so vast or so identical, for humans are humans. I don't think I answered your question, Art. Sorry."

"You did, because this is a world that passes by us; other than the news we read. We know very little about it. It is like their world does not exist if parallel with our society."

"Art you said something I meant to include in my homily. I said if needed I would be on the street with Sam for some rescue. I would and I will. Still, after that, I will be able to come to my own bed and have a cup of tea. Like returning to my comfort zone -- some qualified comfort, but comfort."

"Outstanding narrative, Fausto. Now, on Sam but on a trivial note. Do you still act as Sam's bank, holding his money?" asked Max.

"Oh, no. Actually, it happened only for a short period of time. I got a checking account for him free of monthly charges. I saw an ad in the paper that one regional bank was offering checking accounts with no service charges for life and got one for him. He is disciplined with the management of ins and outs and consults me. And, about the

188

deal of safe keeping his money, I told him that in spite of the Catholic Church being so friendly, one had to avoid appearances of impropriety. He understood it. And another thing -- Sam also makes money besides the small benefits from the City. His side jobs are indicative of the respect he gets from downtown people."

"Such as what?" asked Arthur.

"Such as a downtown courier -- carrying packages from one firm to another. There are a ton of small legal firms, small investment advisors and other niches. The Internet even with emails and faxes are not enough. That is sweet money on the side. His work in downtown San Francisco is faster than UPS."

"I get it. So, what is next after Randolph is gone?" asked Walter.

"Sam is making good use of the shelter, as a day overseer? Isn't that it, Herb?" Herb nodded. "He still visits the streets; finds homeless people he can convert to good habits -- like from drugs. Drug users are tough to handle because the users lie all the time. But he helps transient homeless and directs them to move on to the outer areas in the Bay Area or comforts them with words. He will find someone to fill Randolph's void. He will. Yet difficult, for Randolph, who is twenty years younger than him, was a real find. Three years with Sam, both would clean dozens of people a year; they were that good. Sam will find a replacement; it will take time. He is patient now."

"Let's stretch our legs. I am going to see your vegetable garden," claimed Max.

"Go, get some green beans and fava beans. They are about ready. Vera will get you a bag." Walter replied.

∞∞∞∞∞

Meanwhile the ladies were having a ball with Sam. "Your friend Randolph is leaving you. You will miss him." Said Karen.

"I will. But he is doing the right thing; he has helped many people."

"He is much younger than you; however, I thought he was hooked on you," stated Elvera.

Sam added, "that is true and also the reason he needed to find new places. He needed to live his other journey in life. It worked so well. I will always remember him and wish him the best. I am certain he will achieve the best for himself."

"Where is he going?" prompted Katheryn.

"Somewhere around Houston. His girlfriend is returning home. Let me think -- not really, but close to where her parents live. Her brother had insisted in telling her that her parents forgave her and were willing to take her back. She'll go back but not to live with them."

"Long story. And Randolph is in the loop!" ventured Karen.

"Good read. You are smart. Being a writer, you can decipher the game."

Karen smiled, nodded a "thank you" and hoped Sam would continue. He did: "Randolph was like a son to me. He got himself out of drugs and together we did get as many people as we could free of the drug evil. Sally, his girlfriend, was one of them who got out of drugs. Then, she became like him -- two peas in a pod. They would listen to the homeless stories -- I mean young homeless in drugs -- play the game with them and then apply the realities of life." Sam was interrupted by Karen with a question ... as what life. Sam replied ... "realities of life means that is the way it should happen -- live a decent life. People need help, need to see the light. And, they also believe people can turn their lives around."

"So, you and Randolph, and ... Sally were the light," added Katheryn.

"Many of us are that light."

"Then, Randolph and Sally worked in pairs, right?" Karen continued as if ready to collect information for her essay or book. Instead, she braved a question that had lingered in her mind. "Pardon me, Sam. You speak so well, as if you had a good education."

Sam blushed and thanked Karen. "Not much more than high school." He paused and found his better answer. "You see, when I got clean and changed my ways, I started reading the papers daily, you see, discarded papers. Then I came to spend some time in the library. It helped. Father Mancini noticed some changes in my conversation and encouraged me to stay informed and to read when I could." He paused while Karen processed the explanation -- in awe. Sam continued: "It is not a big deal."

"Sorry, Sam, it is a big deal. To me it is. Do you have a cell phone?"

"I do. Under Obama's rules we got cell phones for free. You know, discarded phones. And, we could get service almost for free through the libraries. However, I do not make that much use of it. It could become a vice."

"Thanks, Sam, and sorry for interrupting your story. Go on, if you remember," finished Karen.

Sam smiled and relieved of more questions; actually, he was anxious to finish his stories. "I know you are a writer and that is fine. Let me tell you a couple more stories. When I came to know Sally, Randolph was experienced with girls. He was always with girls or girls would tag along with him. That made me think he was directing them to night clubs, not as a pimp; I swear. It is that he has some charm -- homeless charm, if you understand what I mean. All for the good, because he would bring them where I was and then we would work on their weaknesses. Most of it was about family, family problems, generation problems and conflicts. Then, we would give them a choice -- live like us, without responsibilities of paying rent, bills, job obligations and sleeping under the stars, in the rain. Drugs lead to trouble, and they knew the repercussions. Once they listened to us and we suggested changes, they started finding good alternatives. When we thought they were ready, we shipped them back to where they had come from. Many times, Randolph and I got them cleaned up, dressed them with good used clothes and gave them some money for a three-day bus trip. Father Mancini helped us with clothes and whatever."

Sam stopped as the three ladies just listened with keen attention. "I am happy for Sally and Randolph. Her brother says she has a job waiting for her. Sally has pop — she can wait on tables, do bartender work, or anything. She needs a break and motivation, a purpose." The ladies were still in listening mode; Sam thought of finishing the narrative. "Randolph will be working on a small farm and having the use of a modest house for free. Randolph and Sally can make it; they will make it."

"How about you?" Braved Elvera, finally.

"I will make it, too. I am here. I understand now that you are my friends, and also feel destined to do what I am doing in a smarter way. I am happy. I will find other Randolphs and Sallys."

Tears were slowly dropping on their cheeks. Sam said he was going to the bathroom.

9

Karen does her magic

Shares her recollections

----

*With **integrity**, you have nothing to fear,*
since you have nothing to hide.
With integrity, you will do the right thing.
So, you'll have no guilt!
-----Zig Ziglar

Karen was determined to write about her experience acquired at the professor's project and above all about the mountain of stories and vignettes she came to unpretentiously and unsuspectedly collect at Elvera's barbecue party. Her experience in several recent consecutive trips to Africa, South and Central America, Far East but less known countries like Nepal, Brunei, Mongolia, Sri Lanka, were the base and raw material for another writing mission. These stories were obtained at marginal places but with plenty of human value. Her stories would also be syndicated in second tier publications; less popular magazines -- lesser pull than Vogue, Vanity Fair, Playboy and the like. The magazines or periodicals were more regional than global.

Granted, she had received several meaningful accolades, but she earned no writers' prizes. Moreover, her little pay was no match to her love for research and subsequent stories -- her true recompense.

Karen, now with new vigor, planned to avail herself of referrals or directions gleaned from her friends' references to swim in a matter very dear to her -- *follow the immense trail of poverty*. Or, a matter that accidentally exploded in her mind and disrupted her soul. Her writing skills would be tested again as much as her sensitivities. It was a call that presented many aspects similar to the ones she had come to experience a few months back. Her planned undertaking now required very little traveling, but a similar agony with basically similar protagonists dealing with life on the fringes, life underground, under the stars, under the thin possibilities of life and death. She was happy. She was ready, for her finished world-wind trips were now retired news of a recent past. She was aware it would be same old same with new blood. *How nice! Perhaps poignant.* She surmised.

Prior to meeting her yet-to-be-targeted subjects, she mapped out what more she needed to learn. What would be fact or fantasy, dressed heroism on emotionally forced events, or just realities that all sectors of society prefer not to know or wished to take a pass. She had to have face-to-face encounters, and none close to hit and run assignments. After all, these would provide the nourishment, the vitamins for a relevant writing project. Meetings with Fausto, Herbert, Elvera or, in more detail, with Sam, would validate her research, her findings, and her prize stories.

Before these potential chats with her friends, she planned to visit or help in soup kitchens, learn from shelters, help in second hand thrift stores, food banks and the amalgamated number of organizations supposedly dedicated to help in the have-nots or those having very little. And (this big and valuable *and*) invest real time with the protagonists of the stories. Sam had unequivocally told her that without smelling the ghettos' flavors, the street homeless' trials and tribulations, her stories would be second-hand stories or stories devoid of sweat, heart and soul, and having no tears. She remembered Sam telling her: "I can help or lead you. Yet, the stories need to be lived and not relayed. You need to dirty your hands, ask your questions, spill your heart on the interlocutors." When Karen questioned such risk of too close for comfort encounters, Sam would tell her, nicely but candidly, to stay home; or instead, "enroll your husband on the riskier escapades." Fausto, likewise, would confirm that Sam was correct. He would confirm that, many years back, he found Sam on the streets, slept a few short nights on the streets, side-by-side with him, and only then, earned the right to Sam's invisible love and respect.

"Karen, everything worth risking delivers great results; not faked stories a la Geraldo's." That was another phrase she had learned from Fausto -- a juxtaposition of Sam's sentiments.

∞∞∞∞∞

Karen was ready to roll up her sleeves and embark on her odyssey that somehow would parallel the project that she had just finished. However, there were subtle, remarkable and profound differences or information gathering traps. While her past research dealt with people with little participation in the meager and perennial economic landscape of the countries she covered, the people she was targeting now were also marginalized -- almost irremediably marginalized, practically and metaphorically in her backyard. The difference, as she saw or anticipated the trap, centered on the fact that those who were cast off lived in a country of plenty -- the U.S. of A. Researching a country where poverty status represented seventy percent of the total population, the next twenty-five percent, the obedient enforcers of the system, and the rest the dictator and the ruling class of the system, is somewhat black and white. That was their system -- right or wrong. The question then would be why are things this way? Why is there systemic but mandated poverty? Why did ancient systems still exist in the 21st century? Why is there the perpetual enslavement of human beings? Why? But Karen knew the rules of the game. Karen also knew that without help, trickled down help from the western civilization, poverty would be poverty in these countries that sometimes-mirrored levels close to a makeshift holocaust. Her research with lofty mandates for answers to eternal questions would not deviate that much from the established facts.

Karen also learned that poverty in the world, after all, had been reduced in appreciable numbers. If many -- like a billion thru three -- were still left behind, reliable statistics revealed that great Samaritans from the West had been pouring vast amounts of money, know-how, and good will towards reducing the very ugly numbers of *have-nots*. Some progress had been achieved, she conceded. Still, Karen decided to devote more time in corroborating these numbers and matching them to on-going strategies towards a more equitable spread of economic rewards.

Now, homelessness in America was another story for the landscape produced lots of bees, lots of honey bees, but lots of bee distribution disparities. There is no comparison. No matter what measuring sticks she utilized. At the early stages of her project, she claimed with much authority, it would surely be much better being poor in the countries she covered so far than on the streets of San Francisco, Oakland, New York or elsewhere in the big urban centers. It is much better, for there are less ignoble status and living conditions. Can one see living in the middle of economic paradise with no access to breathing space and conditions? Can one see a nearby river with running honey and no strength to stretch one's arms to catch a drip, a drop, or even the smell? So sad, she concluded. No, she would not give up the research. *No siree!* She had to find the moral strength and the joy of writing such a piece. After all, she was sure that many stories or projects like the one she was about to take on, had been adequately produced and relayed to millions of readers hungry for dramatic print. Or viewers attentive to documentaries and short TV stories. Hers would not involve unique strategies and dramatic results. Likewise, she still remembered or had her memory bank duly stored with utterances of "redistributions of wealth" attributed to socialism, or communist countries that became a non-event. She knew quite well the sources of these utterances; for some of these came from some of her own acquaintances.

Karen's research would take her to many sources of information about social justice in the United States. She had previously done research relating to the basic role of the United Nations and their measurable accomplishments in a world of finger pointing and politics, to big brother countries leveraging their power and the inherent chances of survival. In spite of the world's acceptance that little is better than nothing, the UN, as universally assailed, was living on borrowed time. The economic giant, the USA, was bitching too much lately, and the political rigid regimes of Russia and China stood ready to apply their ideological tools towards carving more say on the destinies of countries comfortable with perennial poverty. Karen knew this all.

∞∞∞∞∞

Okay Karen, you know the system, you know the politics, you have seen the scenes, the TV reports and videos, and now you also know those who are close to the matter: "What else do you need to know?" she muttered to herself.

What do you know about your neighbors, your community, their habits, their generosity, their bigotry, their beliefs? What do you know that can substantiate or back the colors you want to reveal in your finished product? Yes, the environments at your church. Are your friends' tendencies closer to help or apathy; are they more politically inclined or make-no-waves is better, is safer? What do I finally believe, or what resolve do I possess to make a difference? Did the gathering at Elvera's barbecue cause me to move from a neutral position to one of taking charge?

Karen thought she was ready to make the cut, to turn the corner or walk the walk, to put the metal to the pedal. *Let me update my resolve by listing ambiguities -- ambiguities in our lives. I must.*

She made a list -- not in any particular order; just in a loose format where she eventually could go through the list again and attach a value number in terms of importance and/or frequency:

Can we be pious and at the same time relevant? Relevant as in relevant to those around me? For piety lived by hermits does have its specifics and personal relevancy.

Can we pray for peace until our tongues turn pink and yet get annoyed when our neighbors' little dog does its urinating and pooping on my grass? Can I stay cool and then impress on our neighbor that the yellow spots on my grass came from an undisciplined pet? Or that the neighbor should have carried a poop bag? Or... a never mind thing? Can one inflict guilt without name calling? Or, just leave it alone!

Can my church maintain a steady ritual while manifesting apathy towards the world's plight; or can it lend lip service instead of in your-face scolding? Could paranoia be compatible with arrogance, hypocrisy and comfort zones in politics?

These ambiguities actually turned into contrasts, where some segments, albeit small segments of our society, kept suggesting that homeless people should be loaded on ships, like the boats from World War II still anchored at Suisun Bay, near the Benicia/Martinez bridge, and then tug-boated to the high seas to be exploded with a remote-control gadget? And followed by a serenade in a choir of happy villains, as *bye-bye baby, undeserving-to-live parasites?* After all, these ships like ghosts, rusted and inoperable, could see a better burial -- burial of metal and humans on the high seas. I confess I will be grilled to the ground if my ungodly coarse descriptions ever come to be verbalized. And, if ears were nearby, I would be dismissed as an unrepentant left winger. I felt good or relieved for thinking that way, though. Yet, despondent for not having the courage to state the right thing. But truth hurts and causes enemies.

This thinking, for sure, contrasts with others who offer honest and heart-driven gestures of help to downtown homeless in the form of hot food -- bowls of soup and sandwiches. Karen even noted that these gestures could have taken a cue from Sam. After all, the call to help was also infiltrating the ranks of the ones with plenty. Thinking that there was evidence of such contrast, warmed up her heart.

Karen would also notice that in spite of the many contrasts and the apparent hypocrisy permeating some segments of the Catholic flock, the church maintained a steady posture reflecting resiliency beyond belief -- in the face of the many mistakes that the Church had made. In her analysis and reflecting the pain that some bad news inflicted in her heart and affected her judgement, she rejoiced in the fact that the Church had maintained its compass, not unbruised, but defying the odds of sustainability. She also remembered hearing that in spite of all of this, the church stayed alive. With too much bruising, it was a miracle, she agreed, that it was still intact, enamored by many and relevant followers. Any other institution with similar involvement deep in society would not have survived. Meaning that survivability was a nice DNA to own. DNA for certain dressed in Divine intervention and support. It had to be a constant.

Even her husband's two initial escapades with her in downtown SF during two late afternoons and early darkness, had a profound effect on him. Seated against the wall, relatively well disguised in drab clothes and old baseball caps, they chatted at will with homeless people that felt at home with this new homeless couple dressed in somewhat better clothes. For the local homeless inhabitants were used to other out-of-town homeless betting that paradise existed in this corner of the world -- a world with many tent barrios or nations. Indeed, the barrios or homeless nations were freely referred to in the same breath as the universally known touristic places. On the second trip, their last together, Arthur vowed never again to disguise himself; for, even innocently, trapping homeless people was not a fair idea.

"Karen do your research as you please; however, I am no partner to this thing. We can be what we are and dress as we casually dress, sit on the sidewalks with our backs to the walls, and chat with them the same way we chat with our friends. The fact we have a bed to sleep in, two cars to drive when we please, plenty of food in the pantry and choices to dine out where we choose, is no handicap to have heart-to-heart chats. Also, take some money with you; just in case. One more thing Karen, I suspect that my experience with your project will not dramatically change my life. Nevertheless, I will ask myself time and time again about the purpose of our life's journey as it is. It is impossible to ignore this experience as if nothing happened, as if it was just a nightmare, feel good at times nightmare." Their two in-college sons, on college break visits, noticed that their parents, especially Arthur, talked differently and manifested subtle changes. Karen, instead, would pursue more stories. Her sons knew that she did that for a living or as a valuable hobby.

She had already understood that the Western civilization tried to amend their take and presence as colonial masters of the past. If these European (on the surface) power houses, friendly and in disguise, turned over the reins of colonialism to the native subjects, it puzzled her, that three generations later, much had not changed. If the colonizers sucked the blood out of the colonized places, these also left the manuals of operable management and wealth acquisition. Instead, she noticed that the only lessons learned were lessons of nepotism, terror infliction, slavery and domination. The apparent good practices of government and leadership were buried, or favored by corruptive, tribal and dictatorial practices. That the Whites did it, was bad, very bad. But that the human beings of color, of the same race and culture, inflicted the same harshness was intolerable, incomprehensible and inconceivable.

On their last drive home, at around midnight when only a few spots in the city were alive, he shared with Karen what he had learned, what had sunk into his head. "Karen, I noticed you are being fulfilled in having face-to-face experiences. I will do that third trip at dusk, at very early dawn, just to see how these human beings wake up at early dawn or to the relentless noise of cars and pedestrians on their way to work. However, you will be on your own in other adventures. After all we need food on the table."

"I know, I know. Someone has to. Even if sometimes you wish to give up your job and choose something else. It must not be that pleasant at times."

Arthur dismissed Karen's truthfulness with his hand; instead he said: "At least I have a job that pays okay."

Karen quickly corrected him: "it is more than okay. You have fed our family, taken care of our needs. We never thought we would get rich with my supplemental income in writing. We'd starve on my wages. It is just sometimes you're not happy; yours is not the most lucrative field of law. Besides, I sense, you bring home your clients' problems. Even if you rarely share them with me."

"Family law is not bad, and decent money can be made as compared to other segments of law practice. It is just the other stuff that annoys me. Small things, these picky things that couples have, are poured in our lap. And then," Art tried to un-dramatize with his hands, "and when children are involved, it pisses me off that these parents manifest sometimes silly and selfish postures. As if the kids are pawns; on their games of pulling strings. For shitty things; I don't want to go there..."

"What could you have done? Moved from one aspect of law practice to another with less personal involvement?"

"No Karen. We know that, for we casually talked about other choices. It is like any other job with their own challenges. Criminal law or corporate law would never work for me. Defending crooks, or if I were a prosecutor, I would perhaps put in jail an innocent man. I could never live with myself. Helping others in meritocracy cases? Yes. But no money."

"Such as? Helping the downtrodden folks, helping the non-profit outfits?" insisted Karen.

Arthur was now a little annoyed that they were investing conversation on a touchy subject and deviating from the task Karen had assigned herself to handle. He said with some emphasis: "Karen the closest I came to that was in three cases; and these were gut wrenching. Remember them? About incarcerated deportees?"

"I do and I don't know the details," replied Karen.

"We must stop talking about me; instead of your mission. All the three cases involved Southern Europeans that had come to America with their immigrant parents. They came when they were very young, got their education here in America, and gained our culture like all Americans acquire;" Art took a breath and continued, "but went south by taking drugs. Most cases were of little or no consequence. Because they were not citizens, they were let go."

"Where?"

"Karen, to the countries of their parents. And, the aggravation was that they did not speak the language of their parents. How can they integrate there? No language, no integration -- back to jails."

"Well, can't they get help here? Didn't you help them?"

"I did -- for nothing. I mean for no results and also for peanuts -- like a lawyers' minimum wage or for charity."

"I remember that. But the problem, your dilemma or something else was...," insisted Karen.

"Alright let's get out of this conversation. The three cases I took were no winners from the get-go. The money was not the problem either; I knew what I got involved in and helped good acquaintances who referred the cases to me. The frustration centers on the fact that once the deporting agencies decide on deportation, the cases are closed. Even when we use delaying tactics hoping that deportation laws change."

Karen did not interrupt, fearing Art would put a quick end to the story that she wished to know; to include in her project. And, Arthur recognized that her silence was a sign for him to keep on going. "Incarcerated immigrants have limited rights under our laws; they are worse than jailed Americans. They have no access to public defenders; they almost are invisible people. Of the three cases I took only one still lingers in the courts; like I said, waiting for laws to change. Not a bit of a chance now. During the Obama administration it was hard; now with Trump in power it is far worse. You know that? Right?" Karen nodded she did understand. "Now, I ask where are you going to concentrate your research?"

"Listen, I have modified my plans somewhat. I will concentrate on the 880 corridors, for some examples, during daytime, and expand my research and hands-on-facts to Contra Costa County. Vera has said so; I can get good samples of the modern-day homelessness."

∞∞∞∞∞

Karen's plans did not change. It was an idea that saw some light but would not make the cut. Besides, once details were known, Arthur would not agree. Do it right or cancel the effort altogether. Arthur was company to her, instead.

"Good idea. The horror in the city is asphyxiating. In spite of the many changes and support from many sources, the swells of homelessness appear to be increasing rather than receding. I remember coming for shows and concerts not far away from the city center, seeing the spreads of homeless, but never imagined it would reach these proportions. Even Union Square is loaded with them. It hurts seeing such numbers. All children of God!"

"All children of God. Well said, Art. Well said!"

Both in some kind of meditation for a while, Arthur recharged his powerlessness. "The chat with Fausto was great. He opened my mind. Yet, his ideas will never see the light of day. The politics are enormous and so fragmented. The blame game is always on the table. And as long as the tourism industry keeps raking in billions of revenues every year, their bitching just becomes bitching. Nothing else. This will cause politicians to keep scrambling for solutions, for solutions that are within their reach. Yet, these political leaders lack the will to do the right thing."

"Yes, Fausto's own evaluation of the ever present and growing problem has lots of merit. But like you said, it will never happen. It is so radical as the *I-tech* and the *dot-coms* have been radical. One involves new scientific discoveries, money and becoming rich and famous. The other is so Jesus-like; but not fun at all... Too bad."

The chat they had with Father Mancini was as plain as the chat they had at Elvera's. The difference was in the theme; and Fausto was almost like an encyclopedia. Fausto had claimed unceremoniously that government cannot and should not do the job. They should get out of the way; even if others and many people of good will, begged to differ. In his experience, government by its nature of moving chairs, changing what is done by some governments and then changed again by others of a different party, will not lead and provide sustainability. Many people are just lambs following special interests' shepherds, and collectively ignorant of the realities of life. So, Fausto's opinion, also gleaned from experiences shared by Sam, centered on the business, the business constantly and unceasingly coming to town. Only the money interests mixed with human talent, ingenuity and willingness to make their mark in society, could make a dent and become a blueprint for rehabilitating human conditions, and thus destinies.

They continued to dwell on what they knew or read from way back in the early sixties, the flower child and drug happy Haight-Ashbury culture. A culture did surface almost innocently, spreading to the suburbs and then to the whole world. However, their easy-going lifestyle requiring little money (other than for booze and drugs), became the road map for living without worries. Others from other parts of the country, came to town and multiplied. As the landscape and demographics changed by default, the needs also changed. Yet, these were paid little attention. Coupled by the housing crisis, even with rent controls, the problem became uncontrollable. Many San Franciscans left town for the nearby suburbs and from the nearby suburbs to the ever growing and expanding larger suburbia. This was good for jobs, for the economy; but a nightmare in the making. Lack of affordable housing followed, the replacement of low-income communities became an illusion, for rent prices skyrocketed; and here we have a Pandora's box with more ugliness than gems.

"Look here friends," they recalled Fausto stating, "the idea that getting a job in lieu of the welfare was, on the surface, a good idea. However, how could one pay for rent and food with a minimum wage? How?" The answer was that living miserably was far worse than living on the streets.

"Look again. You're very intelligent and must read a lot: nowadays, at this very moment, even people who make good money, more than a big bill..." (Fausto was using a metaphor of a one-hundred thousand dollar note) ... "cannot afford to live here. High tech with all its success, pomp and circumstance, has not helped at all. Quite the contrary -- it has created unbelievable expectations that at some point San Francisco will become a ghost town."

"Then, like you said, the government and business should do better or come up with innovative and radical plans. What do you suggest?"

"Thanks Karen. Simply by partnering government and the new generation of business on bold, on radical solutions. Mandate that business embark on a mission of adopting all the homeless in recovery programs. On this mission, the government would get out of the way in return for the usual corporate welfare -- rich candy bars. If the Googles, the Facebooks, the Apples and, so on, create neat work environments; rightfully so; how can they not put their human power to work and create centers, within or not far from their boundaries, to rehabilitate these living creatures? They can do anything even that which is unimaginable. They could do this."

"Wow! Brilliant!" Arthur remembered saying. "Of course, something as radical as this involves, demands creative thinking and execution. Nevertheless, it sounds doable. I see it can be done. As has being proven, human beings can successfully rehabilitate other human beings. What is it so different from inventing new chips?"

"However," continued Arthur, "it requires the dismantling of the political barriers and a converging of society's views on life, on living, and the reality that we will at some point die. Then, why not create and leave a legacy."

"Here we go, or like many politicians claim, here we go again; another trick to create redistribution of opportunities," said Karen.

Fausto intervened, "I get it. And my idea does not even ask for prayer, for it is not inherently required. We only need to focus on Jesus' great practices two thousand years ago. I mean, Jesus' business practices. That is all. At a minimum, if humans embraced the idea, the graces from above would pour like cascades."

"Well, Fausto, it would be radical; it would invite the idea or perception of 'socialism,'" concluded Arthur.

"That's what I just said. So be it! Americans love labels, finger pointing and misery as a form of legacy. So sad, for we will one day die, too." Finished Father Mancini. "Some tea?"

"No, we've got to go. This has been like going to college, the college of hard knocks," added Arthur. "Still, I am intrigued by and with your radical idea. Can you back this up with some examples? Like examples of bold measures that have been tried before? I suspect you did not study economics with the related rigor, or Wall Street shenanigans, but from what you know and have observed."

"You are right: I have no major in economics, finance and the like. But I have read many books from reliable organic business writers; even the likes of Michael Lewis. I admire the man and I wish he would investigate the matters that concern us so dearly. Yet, he does good work in exploring Wall Street money changers and related shenanigans. You see, I used your word shenanigans." Turning to Karen he added: "being a writer you must have read most of his books." Karen said she had. He smiled as he recognized that Michael Lewis was a well-known writer in the Bay Area -- actually in the East Bay. "But wait. I still did not answer your question. Let me do it. Then I will let you go."

Father Mancini's thesis centered on all the inventions that the modern world had brought to mankind -- from the locomotive and the car a century plus ago, to the not too distant high-tech inventions, to the increased food production -- Father Mancini declared that not all inventors got the benefit or reward of the dollar value. Many inventors did it for the love of discovering new ways to help mankind. Nothing else. Some were left to oblivion. Yet, he slowly and methodically, explained his thoughts in a simple fashion even with some unexpected details validating his thoughts. He mentioned Costco (as an example because there were many others) does not lose sight of their commitment to shareholders. However, he observed that this company aimed at valuing customers and employees, side-by-side with stockholders. And like them, there are others who are changing the music they used to play. "That is radical," affirmed Fausto. "Let us do the same. Take ownership of the misery in the city, not with hand-outs, not with self-serving or aggrandizement. But by dirtying one's hands." He concluded that not all homeless folks could be rehabilitated, saved easily or instantly." He stated that without a fuss. Concluding: "What do we have to lose? Afterall, the bold and the brave would still have money. Plenty of money left over for three hundred million-dollar yachts!"

"Wow, Fausto. Are you sure you don't want to become an economics and social studies guru? Or, a true militant a la Reverend Cecil Williams and his Glide Memorial Church?" Then, Arthur for some reason doubled down: "pick up your energy, rehearse your message, tune up your vocal cords. And bang! Bang! Give them hell; I'll follow you."

"I know you are talking in jest; but it is a vibrant piece of advice. Fortunately, because Cecil Williams is real, your advice has power. But I am fine where I am. Still, or fortunately many respond to Cecil's call. Unfortunately, they have little pull. Attending church rallies is good; cooking hot meals daily and serving the poor is so relevant and lovely. But to make this work or like the man on the street says *catch fire*, we need people with power, strong visibility, connections and the will to cause something transformative. MLK's vision of equal rights caught fire and did lead to results. Something like that of the homeless has to come to happen. Vision and action."

"I know; I know. You have done and you still do your part," replied Arthur. "Who knows?!"

"At the moment nobody knows. But I am fine where I am. And you, Karen -- dear dirt digger but conscience provocateur -- good luck with your project."

"Pray for me, father; pray for me."

"I will."

10

Holy Land in sight

A poetic and final dialogue

Going to church doesn't make you a Christian
any more than standing in your garage makes you a car.
Every saint has a PAST...
Every sinner has a FUTURE!
----- (Author, unknown to author)

∞∞∞∞

Good evening friends:

This is the second time you have bestowed an award on me. The last one was less than two years ago -- in your mid-year award. At the last annual award, you rightfully recognized Mr. Herbert Hawkins -- a very deserving human being. My great joy also goes to the runners-up, my companions in my trade. Randolph and Sally would be happy being here. The reward will get to them.

*I can understand by your faces that you are surprised hearing me say more words than the last time around. I remember them, nine words -- **I thank you, I thank you for this award**. At last I found enough courage to face you more appropriately and warmly. I am homeless, but I can read and write. In fact, I read every day. And like on a few other occasions, you have treated me so well, delivering dignity to a homeless person. And this is what caused me to gather the courage to say a few more words.*

Your organization is so credible in addressing only issues that impact people. Nothing for show -- nothing from organizations or foundations from well-established large conglomerates with self-serving narratives. Now that I am a little braver, let me deviate from your rule of avoiding talking about churches, religions or even God. I understand the purpose or your cautious rule. I also understand that many people live without God, or at least the appearance of God that sometimes may turn some people away.

I need to thank Mr. Hawkins, a Pastor and leader of the very church that founded a very convenient and useful shelter. Now, Pastor Hawkins, thank your God for inspiring you to do that. You know how to contact him. Make sure you mention my gratitude and my name.

Again, by all means, I applaud what your organization does. You kind of started below the radar and wish to maintain your works under the radar. I love this principle because the people I deal with in the many moments or all moments of my life are also below the radar. But they are people that like you, sleep and, unlike you, want to be in constant sleep -- and in many people's mind, that is what we prefer to do -- sleep away our problems, sleep away our worthlessness.

Therefore, from the bottom of my heart, stay faithful to your cause. It works -- one person at a time, one impact beyond words, one touch that lasts and lasts.

Now, this check, your manner of showing your affection, needs to be kept by my chief financial officer. Well, I did open a bank account but normally receive support from another person I trust. I know this person has conversations with God. He does not claim that. But I see him acting like one that does such a thing. In fact, sometimes I get so disheartened with the notion of God and not seeing Him. When dealing with my friends on the streets and, at times, in despair I let my emotions be known, my thoughts expressed and elevate my eyes to the sky and say: Come down here and see for yourself. This is not supposed to be heaven because people, human beings always die. But if you are real, show me -- come and help me. I guess you chose father Fausto Mancini to be your agent. A very good choice!

Please, Brother Fausto come up here and hold this money for me. Love you all.

∞∞∞∞∞

"I'm exhausted. That was a little too heavy for me. Too much raw emotion." Elvera's words echoed around the table of five. Sam, in spite of pleas from the group, opted to skip the lunch offer and instead join his buddies and clients enjoying the warm breeze circulating under the freeway pass or around the Tenderloin or around the Civic Center of San Francisco. Or, go to the homeless camps and parks in Oakland, Berkeley or large traffic street junctions. The five knew Sam's schedule well. Elvera started sipping on her Chardonnay as the others gave the signal that they could not make the day better.

"I agree with what you said. I'm happy the conference wrap-up happened this morning instead of at last night's dinner. Food, in an emotional outcome, would taste differently, or not taste so well," concurred Pastor Herbert Hawkins.

"Herb, you caused some emotion yourself for acting on behalf of Randolph and Sally. Fausto took a pass; and you delivered." Pastor Hawkins stayed motionless and not committed to any part of Elvera's statement.

She followed with: "For my part it was very apropos for the committee to also include those two souls. Very fair! And, it was heart-warming to hear Sam elevating your church's substantial assistance to his cause. Great recognitions. Great speech of yours."

Hawkins politely dismissed Elvera's praise of both addresses. Max just nodded in some sort of agreement while Father Mancini patted Elvera on her hand. Walter was motionless. Like naturally neutral in their interpretation of the previous night's work and this morning's annual conference recap and awards presentation.

Walter interrupted as he meant to cut in Elvera's inspired praise. "Well, I was there last night and felt at home. You guys are real lifers. I am also glad I was not present this morning. It is easy for me to get emotional. However, I am very happy that these two fellows -- Randolph and Sally got an award -- a runner up thing."

"Me too," said Elvera. Confronting Fausto, she added: "were you aware this would happen? They are not here."

"No, I was not. But Herb can explain. He had mentioned recently that those two, quite often, used to come to Oakland. They may have caught the attention of downtown business leaders, and these may have shared information with the Oakland chapter. Oakland is a busy council, too."

"Fausto is correct. Do you remember Sam stopping in Oakland two months ago? Before coming to your barbeque party?" All nodded affirmatively. "Well, Sam knew something was in the making. As we took him home, he hinted that people contacted Randolph a week before he planned to leave town; like that someone with pull would contact him. That is all I know."

Father Mancini added: "Well, the prize will get to them. The conference chairman said that a small ceremony could be held if they showed up soon. Sam should be the one to tell them the news."

"Most likely Sam already called them with the much-deserved news." Intervened Max.

Walter interrupted the story about the couple: "Very good. You guys drive too much drama. Nice to be in good company. Thanks Vera, for pushing me around you all." He paused, measured the others' smiles and meant to conclude his thoughts. "I keep learning about life away from my comfort zone. And you do masterful things like no one else does. I love your company."

Since what she said was significant, Walt did not dissuade Elvera in retaking command of the talk. "I guess I need a vacation different than any other I've taken before. I need to have a walking meditation in a quiet but historic place, an outdoor and serene site, with some meaning. I need one week in free-lance meditation."

Father Mancini was interested in learning more of Elvera's other fine wishes. "Where would you do that? Any place in mind?"

215

"None right now." Elvera thought for a moment and then it came to her. "I know, I know -- the Holy Land would meet the criteria! Another one could be a journey or a walking pilgrimage to Santiago de Compostela. Walking a long-distance journey like a homeless with state-of-the-art-gear, and sleep in a bed-n-breakfast inn instead of on a mat looking at the stars."

Elvera laughed cautiously as the others just beamed with surprised joy. "Or like the writer Paulo Coelho wrote in his short book about his Camino Walk."

"Not bad, following Paulo Coelho's experience. Like he said — sleeping under the stars and finding his occult self," said Fausto. Fausto was alluding at Paulo Coelho's book *The Alchemist.*

"Not really! Well, forget Santiago for my legs could not sustain prolonged and at times physically demanding trails and roads. And under-the-stars is past my time."

"So, some sort of upscale pilgrimage would meet your needs," followed Herbert.

She replied: "I am certain that at this moment it would."

Herbert recharged: "By yourself? No related plans? And like you said to the Holy Land only!"

"Yes, to the Holy Land. Certainly, I can take someone with me," and looking at Walter, added: "Walt is good at joining me in escapades like this one. As long as he does his thing." Walter looked puzzled by the impromptu invitation when Elvera concluded: "Won't you join me, Walt?"

"You've conned me many times before. But..." Elvera didn't let Walter finish his sentence; she could guess it.

Herbert held her hand, waved at her a stop and said: "let him finish it."

Walter thanked the Pastor and finished. "But you cannot con me all the time..." Walter paused for a moment, then continued "... but if they have golf courses in Jerusalem ... or what's the other big city?"

"You mean Tel Aviv, on the coast?" said Father Mancini.

"Yes, Yes. Tel Aviv, that modern town with everything and golf courses. For sure I can be persuaded; you can twist my arm."

All smiled. Elvera had experienced Walter's weakness before. Behind Walter's occasional rambunctious behavior or ubiquitous outwardly bravado he would succumb to Elvera's salesmanship tactics quite well. Or, she would at least find room for both agendas: his and hers. He was ready to make a deal. Elvera said: "Thanks Walt, I was certain you'd deliver. Of course, I love you."

"That was cheesy," added Max with a grin. Elvera smirked at Max's remark. Max now looking Walter straight in the eye added: "I'm a witness to the agreement. You got hooked, Walt."

"Not so fast Max. The final word depends on other arrangements."

"Meaning?"

"That some of you will join me. My golf buddies won't count. They are not as good as you. They don't just sit on the fence. They believe in nothing and know nothing about spirituality or religion; just golf, a good beer, baseball and football. That's their religion or beliefs." Walter's rebuttal was typical of him and the buddies with whom he associated. Yet, most of his buddies were somewhat religious people that rarely ventured conversations on religious or spiritual matters. Secular stuff meant more fun and less argumentation.

Max saw an opening, mild but rewarding opening. "So, in your opinion, because I sit on the fence, I'm better than your buddies.

That's something! Yet, I've never met them, cannot be sure of your analysis."

"Way, way better than them. I like them; they are my buddies. However, the little I've come to know about you, tells me you have life, polite energy and a brain that functions well. Your neutrality has nothing but positive tones." Father Mancini was motionless as if in meditation mode; Pastor Hawkins smiled broadly and Max drew his lips in and then slowly out. He became pale; not blushed.

Walter actually, in rare fashion, was delivering a factual but emotional praise, a fact that Elvera was taking keen notice. Elvera said: "Wow, oh, my Lord. Did you just say that Walt?" Walter didn't answer, got caught on what he said and the impact that it caused. "My Walter. We better stop or the emotion of this morning will return to us. I need something light."

Walter recovered from his own profound words and then asked: "Who'll join me? Any takers? I prefer anyone of you. I have no plans to convert my buddies. Too late for them."

"If Max comes along, I will be one for the ride," said Pastor Hawkins.

"Now we're talking. We've got to make Vera happy and protected from the suicide bombers."

"Now you're back to Archie's comments," intervened Elvera. All knew what Walter meant and as well as Elvera's funny reference.

"It appears that two are pulling my leg." Then, reluctantly, Max said: "I'm in. But, let's review the logistics. Good planning needs to come to the fold. Impulsive I-dos have consequences."

"Of course!... Mine was just an idea, kind of a relief thing, a casual wish after the event's emotions. I'll do some research and find a way to get back to the matter. I'm so proud of you guys. What a team! Wow! By the way, you guys normally play foursomes. We lack one player." Elvera looked at Father Mancini.

"Don't look at me. I haven't played golf since I was in college and when I taught high school. Besides I absolutely have no time. On another note, I'm curious about what Walt said moments earlier. I guess he must have said it as a joke," said Father Mancini. He paused and then resumed the reference: "converting his buddies. Were you serious?"

"Nah, nothing that serious. I like my buddies but have no idea where they fit in religion. They are good people, but, as far as I remember, we never talked about religion, and rarely about politics. That means converting people was in jest; for the sake of saying something." He paused for his answer appeared to be a concluding one. Yet, all were pensive, uncommitted to talk. Then he broke the silence or apparent quandary. "But why did you ask? Don't you believe in conversions? You're a credible priest, do tons of charity work. You must know about the subject."

"I do; and sometimes I don't. Pure ...... confused ambiguity."

"Really? Conversions happen regularly. People have a lot to do with them." Pastor Hawkins remark had the makings and the marks of a challenging question or a reason for some clarification.

"I hate to add fuel to this thing but I'm curious, unless it was a slip of the tongue," injected Elvera.

Father Mancini started and needed to finish the apparent theme of the conversation. He weaved on his chair, recomposed himself and then braved a thought. "Well, we human beings have a duty to do good, which includes being relevant to others. Like we do many times. Yet, people like me and others take credit for conversions that are not conversions, per se." He paused. He read his listeners facial expressions of curiosity, hunger for enlightenment and proceeded with his explanation. "You see, real conversions, in my opinion and experience, do not happen by us the same way as a sales job, as sales people selling their wares. It does not."

"Then?" asked Hawkins.

"Herb, I've come to know you and respect you. In fact, we've had profound conversations lately. Like a conversation we had one time about the Mega Churches and many small churches that left your congregation or the Catholic Church just for the sake that they know better, or had seen the light."

Seeing Herbert waving his hand Fausto halted his talk. Herbert said: "Hear me out, this is funny or curious: I remember one time we were talking about the popularity of Mega Churches. We concluded that these million-dollars, big stadium churches always advertised openly or in disguise that they had the power to convert people. Big time Evangelicals, drawing thousands and thousands of people, and people betting they could buy tickets to heaven. The only thing one needed to do was to call for a limousine."

"Are you serious?" asked Elvera chuckling. The others were laughing with her. "Fausto finish your piece."

"Okay! Thanks Herb. I remember that conversation. Anyway, my inner faith tells me that conversion occurs only when the Holy Spirit says so or comes in. The only thing I can do or you can do or all of us can do is to provide some sort of good environment. That is all. Most people come on their own."

"So, the Holy Spirit is it. I can understand that, Fausto. Yet, the whole world of the clergy, the missionaries, the preachers and whatnot, fill the airwaves, the papers, the pulpits with claims of their feats -- conversion feats. Where are we wrong?"

Herbert's broad question had a lot of merit. The others just witnessed a nicely staged game of spiritual knowledge -- a very friendly tennis match. Max was obviously neutral but also ready to listen to a good rebuttal.

"Well, all of these examples are samples of people claiming conversions in general terms. But when you were referring to Max, I had to be essentially serious. Agree? Max is an educated man; he knows his stuff." Max smiled and the others signaled for Fausto to continue. "I have some examples to cite. And, there is one that stays with me all the time. However, we all must be going; it is getting late for me. I've got some other commitments right after three. Let's talk about the Holy Land instead."

The others did not like father Mancini's retreating from the dissertation. Elvera looked around and then said: "We have Walt and me. Walt will play golf and pray." Walter smiled. "Herbert said he would come and also could play golf." Herbert said that he would bring his wife. "So, we have now two couples and two golfers. It is very nice of you Herb to ask your wife to join us."

Then Max raised his hand. "In this case, I will also bring my wife; she can play golf, too."

Elvera now beaming with joy, rejoined the talk. "Wonderful! Three couples and four golfers. What a gift from everywhere!" She meant a gift from God but held the word in her heart.

Max understood Elvera's unnecessary restraint on the potential mentioning of God. "Okay, we are going to the Holy Land. This will add value to my collection of religious challenges. I could feel the touch and perhaps a conversion."

Silence, almost brutal, invaded the territory, and only Father Mancini dared a broad smile and then a word. "You are so close Max; it all fits in the puzzle and the divine intervention. You owe this to yourself."

"Not so fast. I do not tell jokes. It was not meant as a joke; it was just dovetailing this thing of Holy Land, golfing with folks I admire and letting things take their course. Yes, you are right; it would be bound to happen. I don't possess your faith. I wish I had. Still I am certain I am losing nothing at all by getting closer to you all -- to your beliefs!"

Deep respect and serene silence returned to the gathering. Max broke the silence: "Who is going to get the credit for the eventually-to-happen conversion?"

"I suppose none of us," declared Father Mancini.

The others followed Mancini's statement. "But first let me tell you one thing that I firmly believe and tell folks when they are in doubt." They were attentively listening to a possible sequence of his thought. "Like I said before, you owe whatever happens in your life to yourself. We helped in creating the environment in the same manner we have learned from you. Another fact is that we do not know it all. Many religious folks claim with precision what is going to happen -- who is in, who is out -- forgetting with such speed what Jesus said and the purpose for His coming. We do not know, Max. Or like Walt said moments ago, no one has purchased tickets to heaven. Even the saints were never certain."

Max rebutted: "I understand you being modest and you all being what you are. But far from pointing a finger at any one for credit of some sort, I meant it as a teaser -- to make a point that calls for an answer."

"Okay, I will be late for my commitment … "Fausto checked his watch, then said "I'll answer your need to know about conversions with something that is dear to my heart. Hear me out."

Father Mancini reached the inner pocket of his gray coat, pulled a good size black leather wallet, wrapped with a rubber band, unwrapped it, pulled from the middle what one could tell was his prayer book, unfolded a sheet of paper (folded in four parts) and then prepared to read the contents. "Don't worry, this thing is begging to be replaced, I know ... it is worn but the ink is still good. I have an original, very clean and perfect. Hence, I make copies when these fade. Let me read from this nice companion of mine."

They watched Fausto unfold this delicate piece of paper, now revealing four worn creases. "This is from Father Anthony de Mello, a Jesuit. You see, I'm a Dominican. We have our own following and think we have no rivals. But I always loved this Jesuit. I even attended a two-day seminar he conducted right after I was ordained. Anyway, hear me out:"

A Christian once visited a Zen Master
and said, "Allow me to read you some
sentences from the Sermon on the Mount"
"I shall listen to them with pleasure," said the Master.
The Christian read a few sentences and looked up. The
Master smiled and said,
"Whoever said those words was truly enlightened."
This pleased the Christian. He read on.
The Master interrupted and said:
"These words come from a savior of mankind."
The Christian was thrilled. He continued to read to the end. The
Master then said,
"That sermon was pronounced by someone who was
radiant with divinity."

The Christian's joy knew no bounds. He left, determined to return and persuade the Master to become a Christian.

On the way back home, he found Jesus standing by the roadside.
"Lord," he said enthusiastically,
"I got that man to confess that you are divine."

Jesus smiled and said:
"And what good did it do you except to inflate your Christian ego?"

After reading the parable and seeing his friends almost in tears, Fausto challenged them to wake up. "Come on, guys. Wake up. That was just a good quote. That's all."

"Are you kidding me? That was a return to emotion -- spiritual emotion," said Elvera trying to break the silence and her own apparent discomfort. Max continued to play with his lips in the same manner as when he received a compliment from Walter. Pastor Hawkins hinted a word or a few more.

"That is a good example of the *conversion* powers piece. I bow to your thinking Fausto. I do," said Herbert. "Funny, I've heard about this Father de Mello but never read about him. There is too much logic in it, too."

"I have a few books from him. They're small. You see, Father de Mello's thinking is in line with the thinking of the Far-Eastern religions. It is very introspective stuff. He was born in India."

"I find it a good example of the thinking process for human beings. Do you read that writing regularly?" asked Max.

"Not regularly. You'll ask when. Let me tell you when; it is very simple." Father Mancini gently paraded his dilapidated black-cover book as the others looked with no particular interest. "This is my prayer book. I read that piece when my head swells and my wings push me to fly beyond my true zone. You see -- vanity!" Max nodded and then Father Mancini concluded: "Reading that piece is like clipping my wings so that I don't fly too high; actually, keep my feet on the ground."

"Vanity, clipping wings -- great analogy. So, you said Father Anthony de Mello was a Jesuit?" retorted Max.

"Yes, he was. He died long ago. He was a very credible Jesuit, with that magnetic personality typical from where he came from."

"I'll check Google or Wikipedia on him."

"Do that. Hey, I've got to go. I don't have the freedom you dear folks have," concluded Father Mancini.

"Look who's talking!? You don't have a boss to account to," said Walter.

"You're correct. I don't have one; but a ton of bosses -- the old parishioners and whoever knocks at the door. I don't mind." Pausing he said: "By the way, thanks for the meal, Walt."

"Don't bother, it will be a tax write-off for Walt," finished Elvera.

"Sure, it is. Thanks Uncle Sam. Not really; yet it is her excuse for me to use my credit card instead of hers," Walter replied.

"I'm ready for my trip to the Holy Land." Said Elvera as she stood up, picking her purse hanging on the arm of the chair. The gentlemen followed suit. All offered hugs, with their faces dressed again in emotion.

"This was fun. I enjoyed breaking bread with you guys. Very enlightening, indeed," concluded Max. "Now, I'll wait for your call, Vera. Right?"

"You bet, and you said *breaking bread with us*. You'll be forever in my radar from this point on."

"Oh, oh. Step aside Walt," Herbert teased.

"I'm not worried." Walter hugged Elvera.

Gratitude

Starting with *Simple Wonders* – my first book – I preferred using *Gratitude* instead of *Acknowledgements* or *Thank-you* notes. I still do not know why I insist on this title as a way of acknowledging what is obvious -- the help one gets from friends, strangers that turn into friends and others that become part of the choir of true friendship.

I shared my draft first with my friend Virginia da Luz-Tarver. Virginia, a retired teacher from San Jose State University, has helped me in the past and her feed-back and reviews are excellent barometers for what I write. A few days later, she offered very tangible remarks and "go-ahead" mandates to make the novel known to others. Of course, she recognized editing needs and, thus, at the very end of my journey, she became the *de facto* Copy Editor. I can't pay her. But God will. Weeks later, already in January, I shared copies of the manuscript with other friends and some acquaintances. There came a superb gift from Paulette J. Rishard wrapped in the form of a binder containing a printed copy of my novel with relevant initial editing. How nice! Indeed, Paulette is a true fan and a Good Samaritan.

As some feedbacks followed, I must thank Kathy Knox with the same vigor. Again, besides pointing out the need for a few corrections, her message included wows of "you are up to something, John." Then she added: "I need more of this writing, add something to complete the story." So, I did add another chapter. I had to and recognized it made the other chapters look better. Somehow, dove-tailing Kathy Knox's overview and suggestion, an acquaintance of mine, and a friend of one of my sons, echoed Kathy's appeal. He wrote that the essay in spite of revealing thought-provoking points, also begged for and merited more punch. I heard you, too, Matt Szuhaj. Thanks, Matt. Read it again during one of your many trips around the globe.

Thanks to Lucilia Esteves, a friend from the east side of the country. Her analytical comments were valuable and encouraging. In similar fashion, Reinaldo Silva, a friend of recent years, honored me with an elaborate write-up on all of the elements of my novel. Being a professor of American and British literature at the University of Aveiro (Portugal), Reinaldo's relevance was well noted. Thank you for being a friend and a mentor.

Warm thanks to José Rodrigues for his blessings and wishes for success. José, a friend from the old country, has been a strong supporter of what I write. In fact, I did collaborate with him on a project of his own.

Special thanks to my daughter-in-law Julianna de Melo. By pure coincidence, while I began reviewing the first sample of the real book, she intervened with very timely and credible help. Her vast book review experience came out handy. Thank you.

I reserved my last gratitude for my wife Donalda de Melo. Initially not as visible and direct as in my previous projects, where I relied on a first opinion, Donalda finished strong in ensuring the finished product passed the test. She shared on my concerns and felt that travelling a road of such complex and human impact themes could also present traps. Still, she encouraged me to stay on target. Being a solid practicing Catholic, her fears could be on the money. Now, with many friends providing credible and warm opinions, she must feel rewarded and thus relaxed. She should.

Unaware that the *Self-publishing* and the *Print-on-demand* universe had grown exponentially, meeting Angela Hoy, BookLocker's CEO, was a gift of enormous proportions. BookLocker thus earned my respect for being so tightly professional and friendly. Ali Hibberts, director of publishing services, guided me all the way with great care and warmth. Thanks to all of you. Of course, the cover designer of my previous three books, a friend of many years, came on board as well. Thus, thanks Diane Pierotti for your patience and for designing a cover that matched my book message.

My final thanks for sure are for those who will or may have now read my book -- a real book. I hope it was not a waste of your precious time. It was my intent to offer you a few moments of thinking a little deeper on the reality that God created us all. Meaning all! Not just me. That said, with the mountain of differences we all possess, there must equally be a mountain of diverse opinions about God's tailored presence in each one of us. Believe it! Tailored to each one of us. It cannot be any other way.

Love you all.

JC de Melo

About the Author

John Carlos de Melo was born in São Miguel, Azores, Portugal in 1941. At age twenty-five, after marrying his high-school sweetheart, he came to America and settled in the San Francisco Bay Area, where he has lived since September, 1966.

After a thirty-four year banking career and then twelve years as a management consultant of small business enterprises, John found joy in writing projects.

Among few short and long articles in two mixed language (Portuguese and English) publications in California and Newark, NJ, he published two books and collaborated on another.

The first – *Simple Wonders* -- a book of memoirs and a narrative of John's year of 2011, became his first test. Satisfied with the result, he veered to fiction where he found his element in *Chasing the Dream*. Indeed, this work is more than an intriguing fictional novel for it embodies the dreams, the drama, the trials and triumphs of human beings searching for a better place for them and for those they came to love.

Married for over fifty-four years, father of three sons and grandfather of seven grandchildren, John values more than ever the importance of faith, family and human relationships. Totally integrated in America from the moment he arrived, he still maintains ties with friends he left in his birthplace.

∞∞∞∞

The Author's Works:

Simple Wonders and a Wonderful Year – published 2012	**Chasing the Dream** (An American Emigrant's Elusive Romance) – published 2014	**Untamed Dreams** (A collaborative work) – published 2016	**À Procura da Diáspora** (In Portuguese. A replica of Chasing the Dream) – published 2019

CPSIA information can be obtained
at www.ICGtesting.com
Printed in the USA
LVHW040705241120
672559LV00004B/184

9 781647 185459